THE SECOND POISON

Dutch national Pieter  n part of the Netherlands to a npted, unsuccessfully, to indoct religion. A runaway teen who dropped out of technical college, Pieter worked the funfairs before cleaning and coating oil tanks on ships and in factories. After entering compulsory national service at 19, Pieter was convicted of insubordination for which he served time in a military jail. Once discharged from the army, he worked as a delivery courier and sold insurance. In 2005, Pieter emigrated to Thailand and became a language teacher in Bangkok. Pieter likes to travel, not only in Thailand but also throughout Southeast Asia, frequently off the beaten track. *The Second Poison* is his debut novel. Learn more about the author at pieterwilhelm.com.

The Second Poison

PIETER WILHELM

Dollarbird

 Dollarbird

First published in 2019
by Dollarbird, an imprint of Monsoon Books Ltd
www.dollarbird.co.uk
www.monsoonbooks.co.uk

No.1 The Lodge, Burrough Court,
Burrough on the Hill, LE14 2QS, UK.

ISBN (paperback): 978-1-912049-56-1
ISBN (ebook): 978-1-912049-57-8

Cover design by Cover Kitchen.

A Cataloguing-in-Publication data record is available from the British
Library.

Printed and bound in Great Britain by Clays Ltd, Elcograf S.p.A.
21 20 19   1 2 3

In Buddhism, greed, hatred and delusion
are known as the Three Poisons.

The most destructive of these three is The Second Poison.

Prologue

Camp Anaconda, Balad Air Base, 80 km north of Baghdad

The Sunni sat opposite the interrogator. He was chained to a metal chair bolted to the concrete floor. For almost two weeks now he'd been kept in a shipping container, not knowing if it was day or night, and with no human contact. There were no lights in the cell and a video had been projected onto a wall, playing a constant loop of violent porn and graphic images of men, women and children being raped and tortured. The volume had been cranked up, making the victims' screams unbearable. The Sunni's hands were cuffed behind his back, making it impossible for him to block the sound of the screams, and leaving him unable to pray. In the final few hours before they brought him out of the container, new images appeared, interrupting the video for split seconds at a time. He saw images of his house, and his wife and children. He couldn't tell if he was hallucinating or if the images were real. He began to scream, but the sound was drowned out by the deafening screams from the video recordings.

The interrogator was an expert in coercive interrogation tactics, methods that took days or weeks to build up to a climax. A particular favourite technique of his was exploiting the victim's fear over the well-being of loved ones. Through such methods he'd previously managed to track the location of US soldiers and contractors who'd been taken hostage, and coercive interrogation had allowed him to locate the headquarters of a splinter terrorist group in Basra. Despite his successes, the interrogator's reports would never be publicly disclosed and he would never be given a citation. The video recording he'd used in this particular case had been confiscated from a cell of a terrorist group called Jabhat al-Nusra. The cell had been destroyed and all its members killed before they could publish the video online. As all the figures in the video wore head masks, the interrogator could suggest they were Americans.

The interrogator spoke softly to the Sunni, "I'll go out for a smoke while you watch one more video so you can see your mother, wife and children. When I come back I'll ask you for two favours. I don't think you'll need to think hard about the consequences facing your family if you refuse to help." The interrogator then started the carefully edited video for the Sunni to watch, removed a cigar from his desk and left the room. The Sunni cried out when he saw his whole family tied up in chairs in his living room. He saw the fear in their eyes and a row of masked men looming behind them. The camera zoomed in on the face of a figure behind his youngest son. As the camera focussed on this figure, the man removed his mask and smiled. It took a few moments, but the Sunni's heart sank on recognizing him from the videos that had been running on a loop for the past two weeks. This was the man who'd caused all the haunting screams as he raped, tortured and killed dozens of people. The Sunni began screaming and continued until the interrogator returned to his desk. Broken, the Sunni whispered the information that the interrogator demanded from him. They spoke for some twenty minutes and then the interrogator sat back in his chair.

"You'll be taken away now and transferred to the main jail," he explained. "Understand that your family will be set free only when I hear that you've granted me the second favour."

The Sunni cried, "What could that be? I've told you everything already!"

The interrogator bent over and whispered into the Sunni's ear. The Sunni froze and a guard entered the room before he could respond. The guard wrinkled his nose as he stepped through the door. Two weeks of sweating and the lack of washing facilities while he was sitting in a dank shipping container had given the Sunni a foul odour. The guard marched him directly to the shower unit. Ten minutes later the guard banged on the cubicle door, shouting that the Sunni's time was up. There was only the sound of running water. The guard kicked the door open and saw the Sunni lying in a pool of his own blood, his wrists slashed with a shard of glass. He was undoubtedly dead.

The interrogator received a call, "Hello, Tony. I'm afraid there's been an unfortunate accident."

1

Tony

My name is Tony Lynch. I was assigned to a Special Operations task force at Camp Anaconda, where I ran an elite team of interrogators. Few knew that Camp Anaconda had been home to an interrogation unit. I personally conducted more than three hundred interrogations and supervised more than a thousand others. After President Obama's announcement in October 2011 that troops would go home by the end of the year, the number of US military bases was quickly whittled down as hundreds of trucks laden with troops and equipment headed south to Kuwait. My job description changed overnight after Obama's inauguration. Enhanced interrogation techniques were reclassified as torture so my colleagues and I were encouraged to take early retirement. I'm not too upset about all this, although I'd never expected that Uncle Sam would treat us like criminals. We didn't have a choice about getting our hands dirty. Military retirement is fairly lucrative for career servicemen though, and after twenty years I was eligible to a decent retirement package. The past few years spent living in overseas military facilities meant I hadn't had many opportunities to spend money. My last civilian address was my family home in Kentucky where my father still lived. He was a retired miner who was laid off years ago after the local mine was closed. My unit arrived at Ramstein Air Base in south-west Germany about a hundred hours after leaving Camp Anaconda. The air base was built by the Nazis but is now the overseas hub for America's "war on terror". Largely ignored by the US media, Ramstein is crucial both for drone and clandestine operations. As the most important overseas Air Force base, it operates as a kind of grand central station for airborne warfare. Ramstein was the transport hub for our journey home, as it was for most other US soldiers. Once I got back I knew it wouldn't be long before I'd be discharged.

Two weeks later I arrived at Louisville International Airport in Kentucky wearing civilian clothes, and carrying a duffel bag containing all my belongings. I went to the Avis counter in the arrivals lounge and rented a car for the last leg of my journey home to Hardburly. I took my time and cruised along the highway for the two hundred-mile drive home. It was years since I'd been home so I took in the landscape. At first the countryside consisted of agricultural and cattle farms, but then that gave way to industrial estates, old mining sites and boarded-up mining offices. As I got closer to Hardburly, the surroundings became desolate with boarded-up shops and supermarkets. Weeds grew on the pavements and litter was strewn everywhere. The main street looked mostly as I remembered it. Some cars were parked in the union-office car park, a few bars were open and the police station looked like it was still operating. I decided to continue on to the family home as it was late afternoon and I was eager to arrive before dark. Mining companies had built "coal patch" or "coal camp" villages near the mines throughout Kentucky and other coal-mining states, so many of the former miners remained in Hardburly after the mine closure. My father's house was about a twenty-minute drive from the town. Some of the coal camp houses were nicely maintained by the retired miners with plenty of time on their hands. My father's home didn't look so good though. There were knee-high weeds, and the truck on the driveway was dirty. The whole place looked as if it had been deserted for a while. I banged on the kitchen door but there was no answer. I tried peering through the kitchen window but couldn't see much. I noticed a loud buzzing sound and then clouds of blue flies. I knew exactly what to expect before I forced the kitchen door open. I had been in war zones long enough to recognize the signs and smells of death. My father's body was slumped in an armchair in the living room with a sawn-off shotgun at his feet. It was obvious that he'd been dead for a while. Maggots had feasted on his decaying body, and most of his face was already gone. The carpet was crusted over after soaking up most of his body fluids. I stood there for a few more moments. No matter how hardened you are, it's impossible to get used to the smell of death. I retraced my footsteps and closed the damaged kitchen door before returning to the rental car to drive to the police station.

I was met by a bored-looking officer manning the desk who asked for my ID when I tried to report the death. I offered him my Army ID-card and he gave me a form and asked whether I had already contacted the coroner. When I told him I'd come straight from my father's house he made a call and said that someone would be with me shortly. Glancing at the form while waiting, I decided I really wasn't in the mood. I was mentally and physically exhausted and it didn't seem to make much sense to go through these motions. I just waited to be seen instead. A plain-clothes officer appeared and introduced himself as Harry Cunningham. He said he was sorry to meet under such sad circumstances. He looked worried when I explained how I'd forced entry into the house and at how I described the scene. Harry ushered me into his office and got me some coffee before he dispatched a patrol car to the coal-camp village. Apparently all they could do now was take a look and seal off the scene until the coroner staff arrived from Lexington the following day. Harry suggested I stay at the Holiday Inn Express down the road and said he'd contact me there about any developments. I drove to the hotel, checked in at the desk and then went straight to my room. I was exhausted and can only remember taking a shower before falling into a coma-like deep sleep. I woke early the next morning from hunger as I hadn't eaten since the lunch on the plane. Someone called out my name while I queued for the hotel buffet breakfast. I looked up and was surprised to find Harry at a table, beckoning me over. He explained that he'd returned from the miner's village and they were still waiting for the Lexington forensics team to arrive.

"I had a look and it's not a pretty sight," he said. "We'll have to wait for what the forensic guys come up with, but it seems clear that it's a suicide. I suggest you stay away until the forensics guys are finished and the body is removed. You've probably seen worse, but this is your own father. Let's meet here again tonight once I know more." I nodded in agreement.

During the day I went for a walk down the road and had

lunch at a sandwich shop. I had a few more drinks at a bar than I probably should've had, but then again I had stumbled onto my dad's maggot-ridden corpse only the day before. I was flicking through a local paper at the hotel restaurant when a tired-looking Harry finally arrived. We collected dinner from the buffet and didn't talk much while we ate. We took some coffee to sip on the terrace while Harry smoked a cigarette. The forensics guys had arrived in the morning and photographed the scene, dusting everything for fingerprints before removing the body. They hadn't found any evidence that it was anything other than suicide. Harry asked me to call in the station the next morning to sign some forms, assuring me they'd release the body soon.

That night I didn't benefit from the kind of deep sleep I'd had the previous night. Instead I tossed and turned and didn't fall asleep until early morning. I must have looked very tired when I walked into the police station because Harry poured me a strong cup of coffee almost immediately. He explained that I needed to tell the coroner which mortuary the body should be sent to as he handed me a list of options. Harry then apologized that I'd have to wait for the sheriff's office to release the scene before I could return to the house. That required a coroner's report, which probably wouldn't come until later that day.

I started making the final arrangements. The body was released to the mortuary two days after the autopsy. I just went through the motions and opted for cremation without a service. My mother had been religious when she was alive, but my father and I were ardent atheists, and my time in Iraq hadn't given me any reason to question that. After I collected the ashes, I found Harry waiting in the parking lot, and offering to drive to wherever I wanted to scatter the ashes. I couldn't think of anywhere better than at the closed mine where my father had spent most of his life.

I decided to stay in town just long enough to clear the house and sort out my father's finances. I wasn't looking forward to these duties, but they couldn't be avoided for much longer. I returned to the house the next morning. The police tape was still attached to the damaged kitchen door, but Harry had assured me I was free to enter the house. The stink of death and decaying flesh still lingered inside. I grabbed a shovel from the shed, dug a hole, and then dragged the armchair and rug into it. I doused them with gasoline and threw in a match, creating a tall flame with black smoke billowing out from the top. I'm not sure why, but I then added my father's mattress and all his clothes to the fire.

Over the next two days I loaded the remaining furniture and a few other items into my father's truck. The kitchen drawers were full of the bank statements of decades, together with insurance policies and unopened mail. There was a lot of paperwork to go through and it took a whole day to sort. It looked like my father was behind on payments for his insurance, union membership and magazine subscriptions. There were also some unusual transfers from his bank account. I decided to scrutinize that later and put all the papers into a cardboard box. The next morning I prepared myself for a last trip to the house. This time Harry dropped me off so I could take my father's truck. It took a while, but the heavily-loaded truck eventually came to life and I drove away without looking back. The night before I'd looked up local charities that accepted donations and chose the Miners Charity. It was surprising how many forms needed to be completed for them to take everything, but it did include the truck. Once that was done, I retrieved the cardboard box containing my father's documents from the truck, and then one of the volunteers from the charity gave me a lift back to the hotel.

After lunch I took the car and drove to the local branch of the Citizens National Bank. I explained the purpose of my visit to the woman at the front desk, and the manager invited me to his small cubicle office. Settling and closing the account of a deceased parent is a fairly straightforward procedure, but the bank manager looked troubled when he looked into the account. Funds had mysteriously disappeared from my father's account in the months leading up to his passing. "I cannot tell you much except that the account receiving the funds is at a Hong Kong registered bank," he explained. "Not long ago I had a young lawyer in my office asking similar questions about transfers to the same account. I can give you her contact details, and perhaps she'll be able to shed some light on this." He rummaged through his desk before handing me a business card reading:

Maura Schwartz, Attorney-at-Law
4th floor
300 Argyle Street
Lexington

I phoned Maura as soon as I got in the car. Evidently it was a small office because I had her on the phone within a minute. After I'd explained why I was calling, she said, "Oh – the Thai boiler-room case!"

Thailand boiler rooms

For decades, Thailand has been a hub for firms selling bogus shares to foreign nationals through high-pressure overseas telesales. Individuals with little or no investment experience are approached with the promise of high returns on investments. More often than not, their contact details are hacked from databases belonging to institutions such as insurance companies or pension funds. Most boiler-room representatives offer an initial placement of shares or an investment in a start-up company. Boiler-room representatives assure potential investors that the stock price will go through the roof, but of course, the company (fictional or otherwise) never actually goes public and the share certificates are never issued. By the time the investors realize all this, they have been defrauded since the call centres will already have moved on and changed their name and or location.

In a country far from home, many cash-strapped travellers, such as backpackers or sexpats, are keen to work in one of these boiler rooms in order to simply survive or to finance an otherwise out-of-reach lifestyle. Hundreds of foreigners work in a number of boiler rooms in Bangkok. One diplomatic source suggested that around fifty boiler rooms exist in Bangkok, with hundreds of employees calling numbers hacked from databases or simply extracted from phone books and online directories.

A private investigation firm has suggested that between 400,000 and 900,000, largely American and European, investors have lost several hundred million US dollars since 2004. Limited resources and jurisdiction combined with a reluctance on the part of the defrauded investors to come forward make it difficult for law enforcers to pursue these criminal operations.

Tony

Maura suggested that we meet that afternoon, and just over forty minutes later I was sitting opposite her in her office. The building housing her office had seen better days. The office was on the fourth floor and only half of the other small office units were occupied. Flanking Maura's office were a translation agency and an accounting firm. Maura wore hippie-style rings on most of her fingers and didn't immediately strike me as being your typical lawyer. She was curvaceous and full bosomed and, when she turned to fetch me a cup of coffee, I noticed her fantastic big ass. She showed a lot of cleavage and was wearing a knee-high dress and high heels. As is often is with full-figured women, she was an outgoing and pleasant person. I knew she was a smoker as she had an empty cigarette holder on her desk. She turned out to be very professional and had a file ready and open. As she scanned through it, Maura explained that in just the Kentucky area alone there were dozens of similar cases involving pensioners who had been lured into making bogus investments by overseas investment firms. She added that investment firms in the US had to follow strict guidelines, which meant that bogus firms operated in countries beyond US jurisdiction. The Hong Kong bank account number in her file was the same as the one my father had transferred his money to. From the information she'd gathered in the file, she was able to conclude that a total of about two million dollars had been transferred to the account, just from her clients alone. The Hong Kong bank account was a front; through an investigative journalist's blog she found that the organization had no presence in Hong Kong and was actually operating from Bangkok.

Maura had also determined that the Miners Union was the contact the criminals had used to find potential investors. She assumed this had been acquired through a hack into the union's database, as all the victims known to her were retired miners who'd been persuaded to invest their limited savings by smooth-talking salespeople, only to discover later that their life savings were gone. It was depressing to hear how such unscrupulous people had preyed on hard-working people like my father. Maura told me how she'd tried everything she could but had had no success in finding justice for her clients. I'd been in her office for almost two hours at this point so I asked how much it would be to cover her time. She paused for a moment and suggested that I could buy her dinner and a good bottle of wine. It hadn't crossed my mind to make advances on Maura, but I immediately warmed to the idea. I promised to find a decent bottle of red and we agreed to meet that evening in my hotel lobby.

When I returned to the hotel I upgraded to an executive suite. The suite was about four times larger than my previous room, with a sofa in the living area and a large balcony with a dining table. I arranged for room service to take a dinner order once Maura arrived and chose an expensive bottle of wine from the hotel wine list and hoped it would do the trick. I'm not fond of wine so I got a small bottle of cognac for myself. It was great that she was a smoker as I'd only just discovered that the US had become a lot less friendly to smokers during my years of absence. I always carried a small box of cigars for when an opportunity presented itself to smoke one. After living in war zones for years, and having endured a lot of misery since returning home, I was looking forward to spending a pleasant evening with some charming company.

Maura arrived right on time and we had an aperitif in the lobby before ordering dinner to be brought to the suite. I had expected a healthy woman like Maura to eat a decent portion but she only ordered a small potato salad and a light dessert, which I considered a good sign. I find that women who anticipate sex tend not to eat too much for obvious reasons. The table was already set on the balcony overlooking the hotel garden. These types of hotel chains are very good at preparing and serving uncomplicated food. Maura was pleasant company and she knew how to hold a conversation. She clearly enjoyed drinking and chatting. It felt entirely natural when she said she was going to change into something more comfortable. I waited in anticipation on the balcony with my cigar. When she called me over, she was standing by the bed wearing only high heels, with her long hair loose and covering the top of her ass. It was the most erotic sight I'd laid eyes on for a long time. I felt myself grow hard and reached out to her.

It was a night to remember. We had a smaller session the following morning before it was time for Maura to leave for the office and for me to check out. We said our goodbyes with the usual promises. Before driving back to Louisville, I popped into the police station to say goodbye to Harry and to thank him for his help.

I reached Louisville in the late afternoon and checked into the Sheraton Hotel before searching online for a flight to Bangkok. After a few clicks I'd booked a flight with Etihad from Lexington to Bangkok, via Dallas and Abu Dhabi.

2

Yuth

My name is Yuth. It's short for Yuthakon, meaning warrior. I was born in a village not far from Udon Thani, or Udon as we Thais call it. Udon is a small city in Isaan, the north-eastern region of Thailand, not far from the border with Laos. My skin is much lighter than others in my hometown; in part because my mum is a *luk kreung*, the name we Thais give to those resulting from interracial relationships between a Caucasian and a Thai. Mum is the result of one of the many encounters her own mother had with American servicemen based at the Udon airbase during the Vietnam War.

Our grandparents welcomed the Americans back then because Thai people were scared of communism reaching the kingdom and many Americans were based at Udon Royal Thai Air-Force Base during the war. Prostitution really took off then as girls from Udon were only too happy to relieve the US servicemen of their dollars. Bars, massage parlours and brothels flourished, with some parts of the small city completely transformed into red-light districts. Nowadays, apart from the bars, there are few reminders of that time in Udon, as many of those adult entertainment venues have been replaced by coffee shops and hotels. Such cities of sin do continue to prosper in other parts of Thailand though, such as Pattaya, which still caters to thousands of sex tourists.

With such a history, prostitution is more or less accepted in my village; it's the best way for a good-looking girl to make some serious money. Why would anyone want to work on a farm or in a factory for just a fraction of the money a girl could make in one of the many bars in Bangkok or Pattaya? A smart girl in Pattaya can easily make a few thousand baht a day by entertaining farangs. That is exactly what Mum did when she got fed up with her two hundred baht a day job at the Udon market. This is another reason my skin is so light coloured; it's history repeating itself because my father is a farang, like my grandfather. Having both a Caucasian father and grandfather, I of course have lighter skin than the average Thai, as well as having green eyes and the same nose as a farang. My Caucasian ancestors must have been quite short because I'm only slightly taller than the average Thai, but I know one or both of them must have had green eyes. For as long as I can remember, my grandma has taken care of me and my younger sister, Nok.

Nok is the sweetest girl in the world. I love her more than anyone else, even more than Mum and Grandma. She's mentally retarded, perhaps because during the pregnancy my mum slept with farangs, drank, smoked and took drugs. When she isn't watching cartoons, Nok hangs around the swamp not far from our home, saving turtles from being flattened by cars. She carries them from one side of the road to the other but, of course, she cannot rescue them all; there are just too many and she cannot be there all the time. When she finds a turtle that's been run over she's miserable and can cry for hours while she holds the dead creature. What she loves most is kicking a rattan ball with me and the kids in the village. She gets bullied a lot because of her condition, so I'm very protective of her. I'm a feminine-looking boy; something I must have inherited from my mum and grandma because they are two of the sweetest women in the world. At primary school the headmaster always had me go to his office during the lunch breaks. At first this was only to suck him off, which was how I got my lunch money as he gave me twenty baht each time. In fourth grade he started fucking me as well. Did it hurt? Yes, sure it did, but not more than when he beat me with a bamboo stick like all the schoolteachers in Udon did. Being raped somehow seemed to be in the same category to me. I was a little disappointed though that the headmaster continued giving me only twenty baht. I thought I deserved more.

When I was at primary school I thought Mum worked in a hotel. I had no idea she was working in bars in Pattaya. Later I found out about her real job. She used to send money home every month so Grandma could take care of me and Nok. Thanks to Mum, life for me and my sister was good and we never had to suffer the hardships that some of my school friends experienced. Grandma raised us because Mum was always away, either in bars in Pattaya or staying with farangs somewhere. In our village there's no education after primary school, and my classmates went to work on family farms or in nearby Udon. I wanted to be the one earning for our family. Grandma was getting older and I wanted my mum to stay at home and take care of Nok.

Grandma talked with my Uncle Muk, the police chief in Udon. He arranged a job for me as a kitchen boy at the Emerald Hotel in downtown Udon. I washed dishes, pots and pans, mopped floors and polished cutlery. After a year I was promoted and started working as a bellboy, helping guests with their luggage and delivering room-service requests for food and drinks. This job got me small tips varying from twenty to one hundred baht, and soon the tips exceeded my monthly two thousand-baht salary. If guests asked, I would arrange for girls to entertain them. I knew most of the freelance girls in Udon and they always gave me a hundred baht or more if I hooked them up with a farang. One day a guest asked me to stay with him in his room, and that's how I started prostituting myself. After that, if I suspected a hotel guest was gay, I would smile and flirt with him a bit. Sometimes they offered me a thousand baht or more to stay with them overnight.

After being beaten up and raped by my school headmaster for just twenty baht, I was getting half a month's salary in just one night at the hotel. Soon my night-time activities overtook my day job. For the first time in my life I could afford to go out for a drink with my friends. There has never been much amusement in Udon besides drinking, smoking ganja and chasing girls, as well as gambling on illegal Muay Thai fights. Groups have always gathered in parking garages and under bridges to watch and gamble on these fights.

Participating in illegal Muay Thai fights contravenes Thailand's Boxing Act and can be punished with a hefty fine or jail. Of course, this is no problem in Udon as all the fights are organized by Uncle Muk, Udon's police chief.

The old shopping mall in Udon has deteriorated quite a bit

since the new Central shopping mall opened. Now the old mall mainly houses second-hand computer shops, repair shops and second-hand smartphone sellers. The upper floors are deserted as no one wants to rent them. There are regular illegal Muay Thai fights in the car park on the roof. It's a perfect location. Car headlights are used to light up the five three-minute rounds. The fights are held after the mall closes and the guards get paid to turn a blind eye.

They can also make some extra money from charging the onlookers parked in the garage below. I love to see a good fight and watch whenever I can. When there are no fights my friends and I gather there to play cards, drink Lao Kao and smoke ganja.

Muk

I'm Muk and I run the police force here in Udon, at least as far as you can call it a police force. Our station only has two pickup trucks and ten officers that patrol on motorbikes. Whenever I'm sitting in the station, about five of my ten officers will be patrolling the streets on motorbikes at any given time. Here in Udon we don't require much when recruiting new officers; you just need to have a motorbike and be able to buy your own gun. Besides that, the only thing we expect is that you're not a complete idiot and you know how to handle yourself in a difficult situation.

As police chief I earn twenty-five thousand baht a month, which isn't a bad salary in Udon where the baht goes much further than in Bangkok. But things aren't so easy for a street cop. How is an honest cop supposed to keep his family going on just six thousand baht a month? After paying for school and the groceries, there's not much left, and kids these days have a lot of demands. They all expect to have fancy clothing and the latest Samsung or iPhone. Luckily, the cops can scrape a little extra money together by fining motorcyclists for things like speeding or not wearing a helmet.

Even so, life is not a bed of roses for a street cop in Udon. I know that very well because I patrolled the streets here myself for about fifteen years. My luck changed when my predecessor got caught with his pants down – in bed with an underage girl. He had to do a runner after the girl's father set fire to his car and threatened to do the same to his house. Daddies here don't give a fuck who you are if you fuck up the *sinsot* (dowry) they expect to receive for their daughter. Also, I can tell you there isn't much sinsot offered for non-virgin daughters. Anyway, I borrowed some money from a loan shark as well as from my sister, who works in Pattaya, to make him sign the job over to me, leaving him with enough cash to get away. The rest is history. Now I'm the operator running the Muay Thai fights here in Udon. That means I handle all the bets, pay the fighters and, of course, keep a decent chunk of the money for myself. It's a great venture. Thais always receive their salary on the last working day of the month, which we call *sinduan*. It doesn't matter if you work in a bank or a factory or wherever else, everyone gets paid on the same day. The fights are always on sinduan when people have money to burn. They enjoy betting a little on a fight. I invite some fighters down every month. They're mostly from Udon province or neighbouring provinces, but we occasionally get some in from nearby Laos. Business has been good ever since I took over from my predecessor. Not long ago an old schoolmate who works as a guard at Klong Prem prison invited me to see a prison fight match. I happily accepted the invitation.

Bangkok is a great place for enjoyment and relaxation. It's far enough away from home for me to enjoy the sins I must refrain from in Udon; we are all bad boys! You know what I'm talking about. Klong Prem prison fights are part of a state-sponsored rehab programme, in which inmates who win five rounds in a row can get their sentences knocked down by six years or so. That might sound unbelievable, but I'm not bullshitting. For the inmates it's like a free get-out-of-jail card. It apparently originates from a time when, after capture by the Burmese army, soldiers could win their freedom by fighting. It's a great opportunity for me to meet other Muay Thai operators and it's essential for us to exchange fighters for our own fights. This time a Thai beat the shit out of a British guy. The Thai was doing time for murder. His name was Ma, which means dog. But in the ring he was more like a tiger and managed to earn his release six years early. Soon he would be out and on his way back home to Nong Khai, a thirty-minute drive from Udon. I immediately decided that I wanted this guy to fight in Udon so I sent my friend to find out if Ma would be interested in making some extra money. I was glad to hear that he was keen to come for a few fights in Udon after his release.

Nok's rape hit the community hard. It took us a while to piece together my niece's movements that fateful day. It all began with a game of *Takraw*. Takraw is a very popular sport in Udon and throughout Thailand. This game, similar to volleyball, is played with a rattan ball, but players can only use their feet, knees, chest and head to hit the ball.

On the day of Ma's fight, Nok left our house in the afternoon and walked to the park behind the temple as she often did, to watch a takraw game. A lot of boys were already in the park, either watching or participating in an informal takraw practice. One of the older boys came over to Nok and asked her to go with him to his house, which was close to our village. After initially refusing, she agreed when she was told that the boy's brother had some ganja and Lao Kao, a homemade spirit. He put his arm around Nok and escorted her to his motorbike. When they reached the house his brother was already there, drunk and high on ganja. Nok was given some Lao Kao to drink and made to swallow some *yabaa* tablets (a mixture of methamphetamine and caffeine). Once the alcohol and drugs had kicked in, the boys removed her shirt and panties. Nok was orally raped first and then forced to bend over, with the boys taking turns to vaginally penetrate her. Nok cried and begged them to stop, but they just laughed and continued and then beat her with wooden sticks. They gave her more liquor and yabaa after it was over and left her unconscious.

3

Yuth

When Nok failed to return home, Grandma went out to look for her. Then a search party was called after dark with most of the villagers joining in. First they searched the village itself, but finding no trace of her the search party moved to the fields surrounding the village. There was a breakthrough when a Buddhist monk told them he remembered seeing Nok watching the takraw game before leaving on the back of a motorbike. When the takraw players were questioned, one recalled seeing Nok take off with an older boy. He knew that the older boy lived in a wooden house on stilts on the outskirts of the village, so the search party went there to look for her. As soon as they arrived they heard sobbing sounds coming from some bushes near the house. There they found Nok covered in bruises and bleeding from her vagina. The rapists were nowhere to be seen.

I got the call at around midnight while I was with a Swedish guy, who had booked me for the night. We were just having a beer after a round of bed activities and I told the man I had to go. When he complained and demanded his money back I hit him over the head with a beer bottle. He began screaming so I hit him harder. The second blow shut him up. I couldn't think straight. My little sister had been raped and was hurt. I rushed home, burning with anger. Outside the hotel I ran into Ma Boxer who I'd made friends with over some drinks and ganja at the old shopping mall. Ma noticed my agitated state and offered to drive me home in his pickup. We arrived in the early morning while the village was in a deep sleep. Except for Grandma. She was sitting on the porch. She was calm but I could see she'd been crying. Nok was asleep. The doctor had given her some strong sleeping tablets and she was curled up in bed sucking her thumb, looking sweet and innocent. I was overwhelmed with emotion and felt a strong desire to inflict severe pain on the thugs who'd done this to her. I sat with grandma while she explained what had happened. She had tried to call mum but couldn't get hold of her since she was in America with her latest admirer. I was furious with what had happened to my sister and left, telling Grandma to stay at home and look after her.

Ma Boxer

I'm Ma, but people call me Ma Boxer, not because I'm a Muay Thai fighter, but because they reckon that I have the nose of a boxer dog. What do they expect? I've lost count of how many times I've been punched in the face. I've only recently finished doing time for murder, but I don't think it was fair; it was just an unfortunate accident. The guy just didn't wake up after I'd knocked him unconscious in a bar fight. I've come to Udon because this police captain offered some cash for a few boxing matches. I was just about to leave to do another contract when I ran into Yuth. He seemed upset, and after I'd offered to drive him home he told me the reason. I parked around the corner from his house and took a nap while he went to see his grandma and sister. Yuth had been gone for a while but eventually returned to tell me what had happened. Every man should be able to take care of his own business and I didn't want to get involved as I'd only just got out of jail, but he said he just needed a ride. We drove off but only went a few miles before he told me to park and wait on a dirt track. I don't know how long I slept while waiting. I remember being woken by what seemed like screams, but I just brushed it off as the sound of wild animals. Yuth had been gone for some time though. When he came back he looked bewildered, with blood splattered across his face and shirt and smelling of smoke and gasoline. I told him to sit in the back of the pickup as I didn't want the smell inside. We drove to a lake where he washed and changed into some of my clothes before I dropped him off at the hotel and went on my way.

Muk

The stilted house had been on fire, and the gas tank of the motorbike parked underneath had certainly accelerated the blaze. I thought I'd better oversee the crime scene before the sun came up and found my men there, standing around the smouldering remains of the house. A few pieces of blackened bones and bits of skull had already been found in the smoking pile of wood. Nothing indicated that they'd died in agony, and at first sight it seemed that the fire was nothing more than an unfortunate accident, most likely caused by one of the many carelessly discarded cigarette butts dotted around the charred remains. I am a simple police officer and the only thing I want is to earn a living to support my wife and kids, but that doesn't mean I'm stupid. Why didn't these thugs jump out of the house when the fire took hold; were they very drunk or high? I don't think so! I suspect they were already dead before the fire started. But we all knew what those burned thugs had done.

We just blamed the fire on a discarded cigarette butt as none of us was keen to explore or even suggest an alternative scenario.

Grandma

Many years ago I spent a lot of time in bars with American servicemen. I was the regular girl of a fighter pilot who flew out each day to some poor village in Vietnam to sow death and destruction. I'm sure it destroyed his soul because his green eyes were always cold and cruel. I try very hard to forget what this evil man took pleasure in doing to me. Unfortunately, it all came back to me when my daughter gave birth. From between her legs I found those same evil green eyes staring back at me. I'm an ordinary woman and I couldn't comprehend how I could see those same evil eyes again, so I ran to the temple and threw myself on the ground to pray to Buddha, but I couldn't! I was crying so loudly that the monks woke the abbot who ran over to comfort me. Buddhist monks cannot touch women, you know, but he chanted prayers until my sobs receded, and only then could I tell him how the American warrior had returned to my family. The abbot listened and seemed concerned. He explained that under the sway of karma, most of us are drawn back to life by destructive emotions and desires. He was referring specifically to the second poison, which is the destructive emotion of hate. He urged me not to hate my new-born grandson. When I eventually returned home hours later, I told my daughter that her son should be named Yuthakon, which means warrior. Many years have passed since then, and over the years Yuth turned out to be a nice, softly spoken and quiet boy. Today though, I saw that look of evil in his eyes which I'd seen so many times before in his grandfather's eyes.

4

Yuth

My uncle, Muk, paid me a visit a few days after Nok's rape. We sat in the shade of a tree behind the hotel and talked, or rather, he spoke. He didn't mention the fire but told me that Ma Boxer had phoned from Pattaya about a job waiting for me. He handed me a bus ticket. It was obvious that he wanted me out of the way. I got on the night bus to Pattaya that same day, and started working as a prostitute in a bar called Boyz Boyz, the oldest gay bar in Pattaya's gay nightlife district. The area is full of places catering to gays, from bars and massage shops to restaurants and guesthouses. I don't think I'm gay because I keep getting paid by farang couples to fuck them both, and I have absolutely no problem with that. A fresh young farm boy can make good money in Pattaya. So long as you don't limit yourself too much that is. Competition is strong so we have to fight for every customer, and you can't refuse many of the farangs' perverted demands because they'll just move on to the next boy. Some of them wanted to get rough with me and tie me up and play rape games. A short time with a farang will earn me five hundred baht. I can get a thousand if I sleep with him in his hotel, and weird and kinky stuff will pay even more. Pattaya is a magnet for poor and uneducated boys and girls from Isaan. I've been fascinated by the ladyboys ever since I arrived in Pattaya. I've seen them hanging around on Beach Road and behind Soi 6. They're extremely attractive and very feminine in appearance. I got to know one of them as we were both booked for a threesome with a German guy. I was impressed by the ladyboy's body, her long black silky hair and her beautiful boobs. I wanted to know more about her, and so after the encounter I went for a drink with her.

US Bureau of Democracy, Human Rights and Labor
Thailand's Dark Side Papers

In the USA and many other western countries it has only recently become acceptable to support and stand up for the LGBT community. In Thailand, however, ladyboys have been present for hundreds of years, with images of transsexual women being found from the 19th century. In Thailand this isn't a modern phenomenon. Most ladyboys refer to themselves as phuying *(women), with only a few referring* to *themselves as* katoi *or "third gender", a socially accepted gender in Thailand. Katoi is of Khmer origin and is often used in English conversation with Thais. Katoi are numerous in Thailand and are seemingly accepted by society, likely because Thai Buddhism doesn't specifically regard homosexuality as a sin and there are no specific prohibitions against it. More recently, a new phenomenon has arisen in Thailand where straight men have begun entertaining foreign tourists in gay clubs or having sex-change operations to enter the lucrative transgender sex industry. Preliminary steps are not required to undergo hormone treatment and sexual realignment surgery in Thailand, and there are also none of the mandatory psychiatric evaluations required in the West. Many men decide against having an operation and instead grow their breasts and grow some feminine curves naturally using hormones, although more often than not this makes their penis non-functional. This is the primary reason that many opt for breast implants to keep their penis fully functional, which is certainly more useful from a commercial perspective. Westerners, and more recently Middle Eastern men, prefer a versatile ladyboy who can act as both a male and a female during their sexual encounter. These ladyboys try to appear as typical Thai women with long hair to signify their feminine beauty. The other type of ladyboy consists of men who have undergone hormone treatment in conjunction with their penis removed and reconstructed into a vagina. These men consider themselves as fully female and are not primarily driven by commercial interests. Although many of this group are also active in the sex industry, they often serve heterosexual men. Most men who knowingly buy sex from ladyboys are either homosexuals in denial or bisexual. Most of them don't think of ladyboys as homosexuals or men, but they are specifically attracted to "that extra special something down there". When asked, one westerner said, "I am happy with my ladyboy girlfriend. I love her as woman, I love her femininity and people can't even tell that my girlfriend is a ladyboy because she is so feminine." Another westerner was more straightforward: "a dick is definitely not a female sex organ! You can't be a straight man if you like Ladyboys."*

The Economics

The US Department of Democracy, Human Rights, and Labor reported in 2015 that there were between 600,000–800,000 sex workers in Thailand, while current statistics point to there being between 800,000 and 2 million sex workers in the country. The Thai prostitution industry generates over $6.4 billion a year in revenue, accounting for roughly ten percent *of the country's GDP. However, the report doesn't cover the proportion of the total revenue generated by transgender people working in the Thai sex industry. Additionally, related revenues generated by sex tourists in the food and hospitality industries are not taken into account. Simply put, most hotels including those belonging to international chains would not exist in Thailand without the revenue generated by sex tourism.*

Yuth becomes Yayee

On turning eighteen, I decided to have a partial sex-change operation. I grew my hair long and got myself a nice pair of fake boobs. Cutting my dick off was never an option in my mind – that's my best money-maker. I didn't take any hormones either because there's not enough Viagra in the world to keep a ladyboy's cock hard while taking hormones. The whole thing was a bargain at only 15,000 baht. I needed a female name to go with it and so I called myself Yayee. Working as a ladyboy in Pattaya was a whole different ball game. There are some ladyboy bars on Soi 6 with short-time rooms upstairs, but I spent most of my time hanging around Walking Street – the main red-light district – or in discos, and of course on Beach Road, where there's a sort of human-flesh market. On Beach Road sex can be bought from underaged and older male and female hookers. Beach Road has its own ladyboy scene between Soi Praisanee and the Royal Garden Mall.

Guys buying sex from me as a ladyboy cared more about my appearance compared to my previous gay customers. Many got really turned on by me parading naked around their hotel room wearing only high heels and an erection. The sex was the same though; they only wanted to get sucked and fucked. I got to know a lot of the other ladyboys plying their trade on the streets, and my new friends were often involved in theft and robberies. Many specialized in swiping cash and bank cards, which isn't difficult when their customers are in the shower or have had their drinks surreptitiously spiked. Older ladyboys who struggle to find new customers specialize in pickpocketing and snatching gold chains in drive-by robberies. On any given night the bars are filled with farangs, many of them Pattaya regulars. The regulars usually take a taxi from Suvarnabhumi Airport in Bangkok straight to Pattaya, and rarely go anywhere else in Thailand.

They're not difficult to spot as they're often fat; they wear gold chains and are usually covered in tattoos. They can be found loudly and drunkenly sharing their fatheaded opinions with anyone in earshot. These farangs think they know it all, but at some point they'll finally realize how they couldn't have been more wrong! Sometimes they insult the girls or get rough with them while they're in a short-time room. This kind of behaviour isn't wise in Pattaya; bargirls will send us a text to tell us when one of these farangs leaves a bar or short-time room to drunkenly wander the streets. We just drive by on a motorbike and either rip the gold chains from their necks or beat them up before relieving them of their valuables. We share some of the loot with the girls who tip us off to ensure they'll do the same for us the next time. We occasionally get caught by the police, but the gold and other valuables are rarely returned to their owner. We keep everything we take from the farangs. It's fair if you consider all the disgusting things they make us do, plus we aren't the only ones ripping them off. I don't give a fuck – they're animals!

About a year after I started working as a ladyboy I met a girl who'd just arrived in Pattaya from Bangkok. She approached me while I was having a quick snack in the Royal Garden Mall, which is a great spot to pick up customers when you're fed up with cruising the streets. She told me her name was Nid and that she had a regular customer coming from the US who wanted a threesome with Nid and a ladyboy. He had already sent her the money to rent a condo and to find a suitable ladyboy. She offered me ten thousand baht to join them for a day and a night, and even more if the American wanted me for longer. It didn't take much thought before I agreed to join them. She waited for me outside my apartment building in her red Toyota as I packed my overnight bag. She told me she used to work in a 7-Eleven in Bangkok, and that she and most of her colleagues just chatted on internet dating sites during the night. After her hunt for a suitable marriage candidate didn't work out, she began selectively accepting offers for occasional paid sex. She said she was seeing a banker from New York, a farmer from Texas, and that the guy on his way was a university professor. It was nice settling into the condo – the place had a huge living room, three bedrooms each with its own bathroom, and a massive balcony overlooking the sea. Nid set up her laptop on the dining table. I'd seen customers with laptops before and had occasionally stolen one, but I'd never thought of using one to find work for myself online. I asked Nid to show me how to use it. The internet opened up a whole new world for me; I'd never realized its potential.

Nid was a member of numerous dating sites and her smartphone was full of dating apps like Tinder and Badoo. She was connected to farangs all over the world. She explained that those apps are supposedly meant to match people wanting a relationship and marriage, but like everything in Thailand, there is a large grey area. Some of her online contacts had asked her to keep them company while they were here on holiday or on business. She'd given up her night-shift at 7-Eleven and had started sleeping with farang businessmen. Nid stayed in her lousy job in the daytime, and at night she slept with farangs for a fee. That sounded pretty good for her but was of no use to me, so I asked her for the sites that connect farangs with ladyboys. She showed me the more explicit dating sites for my niche market. Until then, Facebook and YouTube were the only sites I really knew about on the internet, but I was soon browsing through dating sites and began dreaming about finding customers online and saying goodbye to my life on the streets.

Online prostitution in Thailand

In the past, interactions between western males and local sex workers were always orchestrated by bar management, escort services or hotel service staff for a cut. The arrival of the internet and smartphones changed the industry dramatically as girls no longer needed to rely on middlemen. Instead of dancing in a go-go bar or finding customers on the streets or in parks, casual dating apps like Tinder, Badoo and WeChat are increasingly replacing the traditional venues for sex workers to interact with potential customers. Now, girls make the initial contact from home. They only need to apply their make-up and walk out of the door after a deal is sealed. These smartphone apps have also created the new phenomenon of part-time sex workers, made up of ordinary Thai woman needing to raise extra money for car instalments or students requiring money to support their studies.

Yayee

The professor arrived late that night and Nid introduced him to me as Stephen. He actually looked like a professor; he wore spectacles and had a beard, but the flight and taxi ride had clearly exhausted him. Nothing happened that night, with him just having a drink and a shower before going to sleep in one of the bedrooms. Nid and I stayed up late. She was a nice woman and I was eager to get to know her better and find out how she found farangs using her laptop. Stephen turned out to be a decent guy too, especially compared to the farangs on Walking Street or Beach Road. He was clean and well-mannered. He had lunch ordered via room service and later treated us to a nice dinner at a fancy restaurant down the road. His sexual tastes were a bit weird though. In the afternoon he wanted Nid and me to wear kinky lingerie and high heels that he'd brought with him from the US. He also had porn videos streaming continuously from his laptop onto the big screen in the living room. The guy had a serious fetish for kinky sex and he got me to fuck him while Nid sucked his penis and licked his balls. When he got exhausted I had to fuck Nid in front of him. It was strange fucking her. Don't get me wrong, I get hired by couples to fuck either of them, but those couples are usually both farangs. Nid was a Thai woman and had also become a sort of friend to me. It was strange for her as well I think, but the money was simply too good so we just got on with it. The orgy lasted the whole afternoon, and after dinner we returned to the living room to watch more porn, but the orgy had already run out of steam.

The next day Stephen announced he was going to Bangkok to give a guest economics lecture at Thammasat University. He gave Nid thirty thousand baht, which she split with me immediately after he left. Nid is an honest woman, and since the condo was paid up until the following morning, we decided to spend the rest of the day there watching Thai soaps, smoking ganja and drinking the alcohol Stephen had left for us.

5

Tony

The flight to Abu Dhabi was pleasant with plenty of space to stretch out because the plane was less than half-full. I paid for an hour of in-flight WiFi and opened my laptop to search for a hotel in Thailand. Because I was arriving on a weekend, I decided on the Dusit Thani Hotel in Pattaya as Bangkok didn't seem appealing on a Saturday. The hotel offered a limousine pick-up from the airport for only a hundred dollars so I included that in the reservation. For the last leg of the flight from Abu Dhabi to Bangkok the seats were fully occupied, with middle-aged male travellers making up most of the passengers. The plane finally touched down at Suvarnabhumi Airport in Bangkok after a journey of over twenty-four hours. Just as in airports all over the world, I had to queue to get a visa stamped in my passport. Long lines had formed at the few open kiosks. Eventually a female immigration officer stamped me in for thirty days after taking my mugshot. By the time I reached baggage claim my luggage was already circulating on the conveyor. A Thai guy wearing a hotel uniform was waiting in arrivals holding a sign with my name on it, and within ten minutes I was heading to Pattaya in a chauffeur-driven Toyota Camry.

The hundred odd miles to Pattaya took almost two hours. After checking in I went up to the room where my luggage was already waiting for me. I stretched out on the king-sized bed and dozed off. Anyone travelling across several time zones will be used to waking at odd hours, and I was no different. I woke up a little before 11 pm and, unable to drift off again, I took a shower. Still feeling wide awake, I decided to go for a walk along the beach and find somewhere to eat and have a drink.

The hotel was quite a distance away from everything and I walked for twenty minutes before coming across any bars or restaurants. As I walked along the promenade running alongside the beach, I noticed some women lingering in the sparse light. They beckoned me over and loudly asked me where I was going. Quickly realizing they were hookers, I continued walking. All of a sudden I found myself in the middle of a fight between a middle-aged western guy and two young Thai girls. I couldn't quite comprehend what was going on; the girls were kicking the shit out of him. After the fight was over I heard one of the girls grunt in a low male voice, and realized that they weren't girls as such, but transsexuals. I soon found out that in Thailand these people were called ladyboys; at the time I was just amazed to see them and didn't even realize I'd stopped walking. I only realized I was staring at them when one of the ladyboys looked at me, so I just smiled at her and continued on my way, assuming that I'd witnessed a mugging. But whatever the case, I learned a long time ago not to interfere with other people's business. As I walked away, one of the ladyboys snarled at me as he continued kicking the man on the ground.

I carried on down the road and was soon nursing an ice-cold lager and a cigar in a small restaurant on the beach road. I took in my surroundings and noticed that guys of retirement age were dining and drinking with girls young enough to be their granddaughters, let alone their daughters. I also saw some couples made up of a guy and a ladyboy, with everyone behaving quite casually as though it was nothing out of the ordinary. Even though I wasn't socializing and kept to myself, it was exhilarating to be out. My body clock felt like it was late afternoon so I continued observing what was going on around me. I still wasn't at all tired when I was shooed out of the bar by some sleepy-looking staff at 4am. I ignored the offers from motorcycle taxi drivers and smoked another cigar as I wandered back to the hotel, wondering if I'd be able to sleep.

She was leaning against a palm tree – the same ladyboy who had snarled at me earlier that evening. I knew I was in trouble as soon as I spotted her. She quickly moved towards me, clearly looking for a fight. I'm no hero, and having spent time in Iraq and Afghanistan makes no difference; in the army you are a team player, and besides, I'd never served in a combat unit. Here I was in a country that was strange to me with no plan and no one to back me up. Only fools have no fear of what can destroy a man before a shot is fired, or in this situation, a punch is thrown. Although I've seen fear many times, I'd never really experienced it until that moment. Luckily, I was able to control it. I feared losing this battle and prayed to God that she still had balls. It was a sense of relief when I felt them in my hand as I went for them. She screamed when I squeezed them. She responded by going for my face with her long, painted nails. I instinctively moved my head and punched her nose with my free hand. We both went down and she began scratching my chest. I grabbed one of her hands to stop the scratching, but she continued with her other hand so I head-butted her and then bit her nose as hard as I could. At this point it was clear that I had the upper hand, but there still was no decisive outcome to the melee. She then changed tactics and played the female card by sobbing and crying out for me to let go. I complied and pulled myself away from her before continuing on my walk back to the hotel. I walked at a more hurried pace this time as I didn't feel quite so relaxed.

Once in my room I quickly showered and cleaned the scratches on my chest. Sometimes bad events have positive side effects. The mental and physical exercise had exhausted me and I had no trouble falling asleep. I immediately fell into a dreamless sleep until the early afternoon.

I've been smoking cigars ever since high school but now it was out of fashion. We cigar smokers are a dying breed. Just as in the US, smokers in Thailand are required to smoke in designated smoking areas. That's okay for those who burn through a cigarette in a minute or so, but it's less suitable for smoking a cigar which will burn for over an hour. Once I woke up I felt a need for a cigar, so I tried to find somewhere that I could enjoy one with a coffee. Luckily I found a coffee shop not far from my hotel where I could drink and smoke on an outdoor terrace. It was nothing fancy, but good enough for me to sit and puff away, and have a strong local coffee that the waitress called *boran*.

I enjoyed the coffee and cigar as I sat, just minding my

own business, until some old, fat idiot plonked himself down beside me. He was wearing a flowery Hawaiian shirt and shorts, with his socks almost up to his knees. The reek of bad breath and pungent armpits enveloped me. He started a one-way conversation along the lines of how great Pattaya was for finding young girls, and how he was able to fuck a different one every day for less than the equivalent of thirty dollars. He also told me about his extensive experience of luring girls less than half his age to his room. He no doubt considered himself a real Lothario, and I'd soon had enough of him, and promptly told the guy to fuck off, which he did while muttering under his breath. This earned me an approving nod from a Thai who'd been watching the interaction.

The event somehow spoiled my mood. The presence of this moron had annoyed me and I left to wander around the area as soon as my cigar had burned out. I walked around for some time and ate some Thai street food before I started to feel a little bored. It appeared to me that Pattaya didn't have much to offer men who weren't either hungry or horny. With the memory of the previous night's events still fresh in my mind, I decided not to leave the comfort zone this area had become, and returned to the coffee shop terrace for another coffee and cigar session. Not long after I sat down and lit my cigar, the moron I encountered a little earlier that day suddenly reappeared. This place was apparently his regular hangout spot, but luckily he ignored me completely and went to sit at the other end of the terrace. I was drinking the coffee and puffing away at my cigar when a stunning girl walked by. She wore high heels and had long black hair hanging down to her curvy ass, but when she sat and removed her sunglasses my heart stopped; it was the ladyboy I'd had the unfortunate altercation with the previous night. Her appearance was different this time and she didn't appear to be hostile. Instead, she glared at me with a vague smile on her face. Presumably, she'd applied a few layers of make-up to her nose as I couldn't see any bite marks. I regained my composure and beckoned the waiter over so I could send her a drink – I'm fairly pragmatic and consider an avoided conflict as victory. When the asshole saw I'd ordered her a drink he went over to the ladyboy in an attempt to impress me with his Don Juan skills. He walked away moments later, tail between his legs. The ladyboy had clearly taken offence at his inadequate financial offer. At that moment I had an idea. I scribbled a note and beckoned for the waiter to send it over to the ladyboy. The note read: "Hello new friend, please join me for a drink." She looked over at me with a puzzled expression on her face and I smiled and raised an eyebrow when our eyes met. A moment later she planted her curvy ass in the empty chair opposite me.

"What do you want?" she asked.

"I'm annoyed with that guy who came over to talk to you a minute ago," I said. "I just want you to sit with me for a bit to show him that I can have you while he can't," I added, offering her a thousand baht just to sit and talk for a while. She smiled and nodded in agreement.

My plan worked. The asshole was clearly embarrassed and settled his bill as soon as he'd finished his drink. I made small talk with the ladyboy, and despite feeling uncomfortable in the company of such a strange creature, the hostility between us had passed. Of course she was pleased when I laid the one thousand baht note in her hand. I didn't hang around for long after that though, and took a taxi back to the hotel. It seemed time to move on, so I booked the chauffeur to take me back to Bangkok the following day, not expecting to see the ladyboy ever again.

6

Yayee

All the farangs I've ever been with have wanted sex, either the vanilla kind or the kinky stuff, but Tony was different – he was the first farang who'd ever earned my respect. I don't think he's a sadist as he stopped hurting me as soon as I surrendered during the fight, and I liked the way he used me to embarrass the other farang by making him lose face – something I understand very well as a Thai. Of course, that doesn't mean he didn't enjoy hurting me. I could see the pleasure in his eyes, but only because it was a way of getting what he wanted. Inflicting pain wasn't his goal. That was the first time a farang had hurt me like that, so it was a bit strange that I liked him. He wasn't into ladyboys or bargirls, and when I invited him to join me for a drink in Pattaya's red-light district he clearly wasn't interested, and left soon after finishing his drink.

His loss – he could have been the first farang to have me for free, but I didn't give it any more thought because I got a message from Nid about a customer she had for me in Bangkok. A Chinese guy was interested in paying for me to spend a few nights with him in a luxury condo in Thonglor. The money wouldn't be as easy as the one thousand baht Tony had paid me, but I would be earning a lot more than one thousand baht, and I was looking forward to getting away from Pattaya and seeing Nid again.

Bangkok

As both the capital and the most populous city of Thailand, Bangkok has seen dramatic changes over the course of just a few decades. The once green and lush city has now grown into a mass of concrete, steel and pollution. Bangkok drivers spend an average of 64 hours stuck in traffic jams each year, making the city one of the most congested in the world. The capital plays host to the regional headquarters of many multinational corporations, and is also a major regional centre of finance and business. Bangkok is also well known for its vibrant street life as well as its notorious red-light districts.

Home to some thirteen million residents, the city's population includes expatriates in their hundreds-of-thousands. Over half of these are Japanese, the remainder consisting largely of Americans and Europeans. There is also a huge number of foreign tourists, either visiting the city itself or passing through on their way to tourist spots elsewhere in Thailand. The many office towers and condominium blocks that make up the haphazard cityscape were built with little urban planning or regulation, resulting in inadequate infrastructure. As a result the Bangkok Metropolitan Region has a population density of 15,300 people per square mile.

Bao Shen

My name is Bao Shen. My family is from Hong Kong and we've been involved in the gambling business for many generations, dating back to before the time that Hong Kong became a British territory. My family expanded its business overseas largely through online betting after Hong Kong was formally returned to the mainland in 1997. A crackdown by the Hong Kong authorities in 1999 forced our syndicate to change tactics, pushing our gambling business onto the dark web. The ownership of dark-web websites as well as access to them is anonymous, and the sites cannot be shut down by any government.

We are increasingly settling bets using cryptocurrencies like Bitcoin and Monero, as the transfers are instantaneous, anonymous and cannot be traced. This fact gives comfort both to us and to our users, who are often from countries where gambling is illegal. The syndicate controls over fifty websites on the dark web and accepts soccer bets for matches in Europe and South America, as well as for horse racing in Hong Kong and Australia among other countries. I'm responsible for a new syndicate betting venture for Muay Thai boxing. Gambling on sports matches is illegal in Thailand, even if the matches take place abroad. Thai news often reports police raids on houses and offices to arrest those involved in sports gambling operations, particularly during the World Cup.

I was never actually meant to join the family business. As the holder of a degree in computer science from Shanghai University though, it was natural for me to develop a smartphone app for placing bets. Gamblers can add credit to the app and can even place bets during a match, with the odds changing in real time. Thailand is a great country to test the app as few people own computers, but nearly everyone has a smartphone. Of course, the app isn't available in the App Store or on Google Play and can only be downloaded from sites on the dark web.

We currently have a problem though. It appears that a *gweilo* [Chinese pejorative slang for a westerner] copied my app and is trying to compete with us. My uncle sent me to

Bangkok to sort this out, and I'm also going to have some fun while I'm here. Not long ago my Thai lady-friend, Nid, introduced me to a gorgeous ladyboy. She is mixed blood and has both a Caucasian father and grandfather. That's probably why her cock is huge – far bigger than anything I've ever seen on a ladyboy before. I'm looking forward to playing with it.

Yayee

This was the second time Nid had set me up with this Chinese guy. He was staying in a huge suite at the Centre Point condo in Thonglor. I've had all sorts of weird customers in my time, but nothing compared to this one. He made me clean his already spotless suite while wearing a maid's outfit consisting of an extremely short skirt and high heels. He just sat at his desk working and got me to pick up the pieces of paper he threw in front of his desk, giving him full view of my panty-less ass while I bent over. Throughout all this, Thai guys would come in to talk business, and I had to serve them drinks while they sat at the large dining table. Almost all of them would just sit and glare at my cock and ass as I served them. One even grabbed my ass while I topped up his drink. It wasn't too bad though. There was a 65-inch curved-screen TV with a gaming console on which we spent hours playing ARMS and Dark

Souls. When I got hungry, we ordered tiger prawns and oysters from room service. Like me, Bao Shen was also a great fan of Chivas Regal whisky. He was a sort of friend of Nid – he'd stopped fucking her, but they seemed to get on well and he let her stay while he went out on business. When he left, we just hung out and got drunk playing on the game console. There was also a good restaurant downstairs where we often went for lunch or dinner, which we billed to the room.

7

Tony

I'd already been in Bangkok for a week and hadn't made any progress tracing the boiler-room operators, but one weeknight I had a lucky break. Due to either loneliness or boredom, or perhaps both, I wandered into a go-go bar in the early evening. The dancers weren't yet on stage, and the place was empty except for one other customer who looked like an American. He was African-American and appeared to be in his thirties, completely bald and wearing gold metal glasses. He seemed somewhat intoxicated but was pleasant company. He turned out to be a US Marine, who had also been on tour in Iraq and was now stationed as a security detail at the US Embassy in Bangkok. I felt a connection with the guy, not just because we'd served in the same war, but also because I recognized the weary look in his eyes that showed he'd seen too much. I felt comfortable sharing my experiences with him and explained why I was in Thailand. He nodded while I spoke but took a while to respond.

"Listen," he eventually said, "haven't we been through enough shit in this life? Don't you think it's time to let go? Your father is dead and so are many others. We've seen people suffer and die, and most of them didn't deserve it. But what's done is done. At some point you have to let go – if you don't, you'll create your own hell." He didn't look at me while he spoke; instead he was eyeing the dozen or so naked girls preparing to dance on the stage.

"You see those girls over there?" I replied, "none of them can give me a hard-on bigger than the one I get thinking about what I'll do to the cunts I'm looking for. To me, it will be far from hell and I'll take great pleasure in it. Anyway, how did you become such a smart ass?"

He glanced over at me, "Hey, I'm a black motherfucker, yet the brass gave me this candy job. They've let me plant my black ass in a fancy office doing almost nothing, and then at night I go out and take my pick from hundreds of naked girls. In fact, you see all these girls in here? I've had them all! I'm like fucking Brad Pitt! And why do you think the US is feeding me all this candy?

"Free rides don't exist. I'm here because I'm now a member of the 'Keep your mouth shut and we'll feed you candy brigade'." I stared at him a little puzzled. "I was in Mukaradeeb," he continued. I heard him, but it took a while before it dawned on me. It's something that every veteran of Iraq knows about.

The Mukaradeeb wedding-party massacre

The village was called Mukaradeeb, which means *The Wolves Den*, and was made up of just a few dozen houses on the Iraqi side of the Syrian border. The wedding was set to be one of the biggest events of the year in this usually sleepy village. Haji Rakat, the father, had succeeded in arranging two marriages that would bring together the town's two largest families, the Rakats and the Sabahs. The first wedding ceremony was between Haji Rakat's second son, Ashad, and Rutba, a cousin from the Sabah family. The second ceremony was between Ashad's female cousin, Sharifa, who would marry Munawar from the Sabah family. A large traditional Bedouin tent was erected in the garden of the Rakat family villa for the wedding-party venue. Hamid Abdullah – the director of the Music of Arts recording studio in Ramadi, the nearest town – had arranged for a group of musicians to perform at the ceremony. The musicians included Hussein al-Ali, a popular Iraqi singer who had been on local television, and his brother Mohamad, who was to play the drums and keyboard.

By late evening, when the wedding party had already run out of steam, there suddenly came the roar of jets overhead. Meanwhile, a column of headlights in the distance steadily trundled through the desert towards the village. The party had already ended and most guests were asleep. Bombs began raining down, destroying the village. Once the bombing had stopped, armoured vehicles drove into the village, supported by helicopter gunships. Troops armed with machine guns then shot indiscriminately at people both outside and within the bombed-out houses. Haleema Shihab grabbed her seven-month-old baby and the hand of her five-year-old son, and started running. Her fifteen-year-old son Ali ran alongside her until Shibab was hit by a bullet that fractured her leg. Another shell injured Shihab's left arm. The baby remained alive in her arms but her two boys lay dead. Her stepdaughter Iqbal managed to catch up with her as they attempted to hide in a bomb crater. American soldiers scoured the area. A soldier kicked her to see if she was alive, and she and Iqbal lay as still as they could while pretending to be dead. Before dawn, two large Chinook helicopters descended and offloaded a few dozen more troops. The soldiers set explosives in the Rakat villa and the building next to it. They left minutes later in the

Chinooks and the explosions turned the buildings into rubble.

The Mukaradeeb wedding party massacre took place not long after the Abu Ghraib prison scandal. In this American prison, Baghdad civilians had been physically and sexually abused, tortured, raped, sodomized, and murdered. Another PR disaster loomed and needed to be avoided at all cost, leading the US army to begin a cover-up operation.

Only days after the massacre, all participants were debriefed and relocated to locations far from Iraq and from each other to more desirable posts, such as the Marine Corps Base in Hawaii, the Sigonella Air Station in Sicily, the Morón Air Base in Seville and the Naval Support Activity in Naples. Many were assigned as security details to US embassies throughout the world.

Tony

I couldn't look the man in the eye. God knows I'm not holy; I've committed enough sins in my own life that can never be forgiven, regardless of what those religious nuts say, but here I was sitting next to a man involved in the killing of children.

The Marine reacted as though he'd seen the same reaction as mine many times before. "Look at yourself – you travelled to a foreign country to do harm, you will hurt and probably kill a guy because you hate him for what he did. Don't deny it.

We both know you aren't here to pat him on the back, so there are some similarities between us, aren't there?"

"I didn't travel to a foreign country to kill women and children!" I replied.

"You didn't come to a foreign country to kill kids, and I didn't go to Iraq to kill them either, but that wasn't my decision to make, was it? When I got there the village was full of dead kids, women and men, but that was after the bombs. The pilots didn't want to kill kids either, and neither did the commander, but we weren't there for a Sunday walk. Do I give a fuck? Of course not; these people kill! They kill because their religion tells them to. They torture animals to death and call it 'Halal' because their religion tells them to. They eat that shit every day and it makes them violent. They kill, rape, and torture, and when they go home, they put their wives in burkas and beat them. So no, I don't give a fuck that those Muslims died. As far as I'm concerned there's only one way to fix the Middle East, and that's nuking the fucking place. And no, I don't give two fucks about what you're going to do with that guy once you find him." After finishing his rant, he pulled out his smartphone and searched online for something. When he found it, he handed the smartphone over to me:

Frank Reitz Corporate Investigator
Threat & Risk Investigations
Company Background Check and Due Diligence
UC Building, 28th floor
Silom Rd. 654/21, Bangkok

"You should talk to this guy," the marine said. I copied down the details and nodded my thanks. We chatted a little more, but by this point our conversation had run out of steam, and soon after I downed the last of my drink and returned to the apartment in Thonglor. The following day I tried to get an appointment with the corporate investigator, but only managed to get through to him late in the afternoon, meaning yet another lost day. The good news was that he was available to see me the following morning, so there was only one more evening to kill. This time I decided not to go out and spent the rest of the day at the Centre Point building where I was staying. There was a complete floor dedicated to a spa and *onsen* (Japanese hot spring), outdoor and indoor Jacuzzis, and there was a business lounge with an upscale-dining room on the floor below. I spent a few hours relaxing in the Japanese-style onsen, and then in the outdoor Jacuzzi while I watched the sunset before getting ready for dinner. As I entered the lift, two women stepped out. I realized one of the women looked somewhat familiar, but shrugged it off, and didn't give it further thought.

The BTS Skytrain was a great way of avoiding the traffic and congestion of Bangkok, and I had no trouble getting to the office of Frank Reitz, the corporate investigator. He was dressed in a polo shirt and casual trousers – not your typical office attire – and carried a slim file. He guided me into a glass cubicle meeting room and opened the file on the table. It contained a report and some photographs of several people.

"This information is all in the open," he informed me. "Most foreign embassies are very well aware of what's going on. In fact, I prepared the report you see in front of you a few years ago for an embassy here in Bangkok. In Thailand, investment crime first occurred on a large scale when the American SEC, the main federal government agency responsible for protecting investors, outlawed these activities in the US. Non-bona fide firms moved to countries that had laws more favourable to them, or more ideally, where such laws didn't exist at all. Many moved here to Thailand. In theory, investment firms here are subject to some regulations, but these are rarely enforced due to the incompetence of the relevant authorities, and of course as always, due to the rampant corruption. The guys you're after aren't involved in just bogus investment schemes. It's not as if they can invest their earnings in the stock market. They also have their fingers in illegal gambling rings and prostitution. The money they spend on paying off police and other key figures makes them almost invulnerable. The American and other governments send out warnings, but there isn't much they can actually do because these things are out of their jurisdiction, and let's be realistic – no one is pointing a gun, and this is hardly terrorism. It's the perfect crime."

He handed me the folder. In addition to the photos and some other documents, there was a copy of the Facebook page of the guy I'd been looking for.

8

Tony

She immediately caught my eye as soon as I stepped into the hotel lobby in Bangkok. I recognized her this time. How could I not; how many Thais have green eyes? Yayee said she was here to service a customer, and so wasn't in a position to talk much, which was fine by me. I felt a little uncomfortable to be seen with a ladyboy, even though this one wasn't recognizably so. She introduced me to the friend who'd been with her in the lift the previous night.

"I'm Nid," she said. She had a fresh and young appearance, and I wondered how she'd got involved with a ladyboy prostitute. Yayee soon disappeared to join her customer in his suite upstairs. Apparently he was a Chinese guy who had something to do with computers. In Yayee's absence I decided to invite Nid for a drink in the hotel bar. She used to work at a 7-Eleven store and was surprisingly good company, well-spoken and well-mannered. Only after a few minutes of talking did it become apparent that she also sold sex. She was exactly my type – high heels, a cute ass and small but firm boobs – so I took her up on her offer.

She came out of the bathroom wrapped tightly in a towel that revealed her gorgeous figure. I asked her to replace the towel with her high heels and nothing else. After a moment's hesitation, she smiled and did as I'd asked. She had a shaven pussy which smelled fresh and her ass looked delicious. In my opinion, Thai women are among the cleanest in the world. Unfortunately for me though, there was no way my cock was going to fit in there, so I made her suck it first and then let her ride it. She spat on my cock and rubbed the head before positioning herself over it to make a smooth insertion. I was amazed at how such a small body could take it all, and she kept her hips moving until I exploded inside her. She continued nonetheless, squeezing her pussy until the last drop. Even after finishing I liked her too much for her to leave, and so I asked her to stay until the following day.

Besides being a skilled hooker, she was pleasant company, as I'd discovered earlier, and had her own opinion about almost everything. When I told her I'd like to watch a Muay Thai boxing match, she was immediately on the phone to make a reservation for a match at Impact Arena in the Muang

Thong Thani stadium on the outskirts of Bangkok. When the reservation came through, I asked her to order a taxi, and she said it was more convenient to take her own car. I was again surprised that Nid was truly much more than just a hooker.

Nid's story: Ten years earlier

The tiny shack was fully exposed to the sun. There was no furniture, and a woman, bathed in sweat, lay on the sheets of cardboard strewn over the bare floor. The pre-teen girl sitting beside her couldn't help much, but she tried to cool her mother's face with a wet towel. She had collected rainwater from the tin roof and tried to make her mother drink it from a plastic bottle, but to no avail; the woman was no longer able to swallow. It was clear she was going to die. The girl was exhausted from taking care of her mother for weeks and there was no money for food. She had to leave her mother alone each day to clean dishes at a pavement restaurant. She earned very little, but each day the owner gave her some leftover food. After her mother finally appeared to be asleep, Nid collapsed beside her and fell into a deep comatose sleep herself. By the time she awoke it was late morning. Her mother's body had already stiffened. She didn't cry though, since in the slum the death had been around her as long as she could remember, and she'd reached a point where her mother's passing felt like a relief. Male neighbours carried the body over to the local temple where monks performed chanting sessions before the cremation. The reduced fee of three hundred baht was waived.

Later that same day, the village head delivered the girl to a nearby Christian orphanage. The orphanage was urgently looking for new children to keep the donations flowing in, and in return for supplying a new child the village head received one thousand baht in cash.

Thailand's orphanages

"Orphanage tourism" is an increasingly common problem. It means that longer staying tourists pay to work as volunteers in orphanages for pre-arranged periods while on vacation. This type of tourism has become particularly popular among young western backpackers. The relations between the orphans and the backpackers last only a few weeks or months, not long enough for the children to form any lasting or stable emotional bonds with the often well-intentioned westerners that are temporarily caring for them. The children go through repeated cycles of getting close to these volunteers only to say goodbye before having to start afresh with a new set.

This cycle is of course very damaging to the children's emotional welfare. Sometimes they're deliberately underfed and given only basic accommodation in order to make volunteers feel sympathetic and give larger donations. There are numerous examples of backpackers that have raised thousands of dollars through online appeals to fund these orphanages. Such young westerners then pay to do sponsored volunteer work that will enhance their resume later. In other words, vulnerable children have become a commodity in this lucrative industry.

Religious orphanages are a problem that is centuries-old. The well-being of children in these institutions is secondary to spreading the religion to young children that are vulnerable and impressionable. Ninety-nine percent of people indoctrinated with a religion during childhood will never change their faith.

Gates and walls often imprison the children inside the orphanage homes. They are allowed to leave the premises only on Sundays when they're expected to attend a church service. During the week, they're cared for by the tourist volunteers recruited through churches or other religious organizations. The children are made to sing Christian hymns and pray before receiving their meals. Religious orphanages were among the first to sell sponsored volunteer work to backpackers and other westerners. Also, for religious types, the money is just too good to ignore. Numerous local orphanages face financial difficulties because they don't enjoy the steady flow of money from foreign religious organizations or sponsored volunteers.

9

Orphanage life

Nid's life changed dramatically from the day she went to live at the orphanage. When she arrived, she was bathed and her clothes taken away and replaced by the institution uniform consisting of a flannel shirt and a knee-length skirt. A fine-toothed comb was scraped painfully across her scalp in search of lice and nits. Her orphanage life had begun.

In unison with the other children, Nid recited prayers before and after eating each meal and before going to bed. On Sundays, the orphans were marched to church for the morning and evening services. Nid didn't understand what the prayers meant, they were very different to the ones she was used to at the Buddhist temple, but it seemed a small price to pay for a roof over her head and food in her stomach.

The Christian charity that ran the orphanage enforced strict discipline and a rigid schedule. There was little, if any, tolerance for creativity or fun. Each morning, nuns came around to wake the orphans at six, then breakfast was at seven, followed by kitchen duties and cleaning 30 minutes later. Classes lasted from nine until five, with an hour's lunch break at noon. The dorm had a communal shower, which was used by ten girls at once and offered no privacy. Nid had no problem being naked in full view of the other girls, and soon realized that no one was interested. She soon caught herself examining the other girls' bodies. One day she met her classmate Tukataa in the shower room. The girl was in the same class as Nid despite being two years older. "Hi, Nid!" shouted Tukataa. A skinny girl with a boyish hairstyle, her breasts had just started to develop. Her nipples were like small dark buttons and her ribs were clearly visible. She was one of many ragged children who had dodged between cars begging and prostituting themselves before arriving at the orphanage. They would wait at traffic junctions with thin pinched faces and anxious eyes to tap on car windows in a desperate attempt to sell their goods. The police had brought her to the orphanage just a year earlier when she was 13. Tukataa had bruises and marks on her bottom where she'd been disciplined for running away from the orphanage. Those caught trying to run away got sixteen strokes distributed equally between the hands and bottom, and administered in front of the entire school. It was a matter of pride not to cry while receiving the strokes. Weeping not only lost you sympathy, but also exposed cry-babies to jeering and bullying from the other orphans.

Tukataa became Nid's best friend within just a few weeks of arriving at the orphanage. They showered and slept together, helped each other with their homework, did their cleaning chores together and giggled at the boys who lived in the boy's dorm.

They were both enrolled in Matthayom, which in the Thai education system is the third school for pupils up to the age of 17. The school provided only basic education, but western volunteers wishing to gain experience also offered some English-language teaching. Despite having missed a lot of classes at the temple school, Nid easily caught up with the other orphans. But Tukataa had problems focusing, probably due to the molestation and yabaa (the drug made of methamphetamine and caffeine) she had taken before arriving at the orphanage.

One night Tukataa was caught in the guardhouse at the orphanage entrance. She'd been sneaking out to give blowjobs to tuktuk drivers to make money for the smartphone she wanted. The security guard had seen what she was doing and also demanded a blowjob in return for free passage in and out of the orphanage. The guard was fired instantly once the orphanage management found out, while Tukataa was locked up in the office basement.

The following morning all the orphans were woken early and instructed to stand to attention in the school yard. They stood confused, wondering why they'd been woken so early. Then Tukataa was paraded in front of them. The bible-class teacher came forward holding a bamboo stick. The teacher bent Tukataa over and she was given sixteen strokes. She refused to scream or cry, but tears began to stream down her cheeks nonetheless. Soon after Tukataa had started to cry, a blond Canadian volunteer arrived at the orphanage a little earlier than expected. The volunteer's innocent vision of orphanage life was shattered as she witnessed the scene. The young woman cried foul while attempting to intervene and stop the disgusting act. She scolded the staff standing by who then moved to physically stop her from taking Tukataa away from the violent bible teacher. The staff pulled her hair and scratched her arms and face as they tried to stop the fair-skinned woman, but she managed to grab Tukataa and get her away, shouting that the orphanage would pay dearly for this. The pair ran through the now unguarded gate where both Tukataa and the Canadian girl were hit by a motorbike.

They were taken to a hospital and despite a broken arm,

the Canadian girl continued to loudly broadcast what had happened to Tukataa. It was apparent to the triage nurse that the swollen marks on Tukataa's bottom were unrelated to the traffic accident, but it wasn't until the Canadian girl posted photos of Tukataa's bruises on social media that the hospital management called the authorities. Later that morning, the police moved into the orphanage, and child-welfare authorities were instructed to take over the institution. The pictures of Tukataa's scars were widely shared on Facebook and Instagram by concerned westerners and Thais alike.

In the chaos, a handful of orphans managed to sneak out of the place unnoticed, and Nid was among them. Having no other clothes, she was wearing her orphanage uniform. When she got on a free red bus she was relieved to feel there was some distance between her and the orphanage. Nid wasn't sure where she was going and jumped off the bus when she spotted a Buddhist temple. Walking into the temple felt like entering a warm shower; the aroma of incense and the monk's chanting prayers floated around, and she was overcome by a sense of safety she hadn't felt for a long time. She hadn't recited any Buddhist prayers for years, but once she knelt down she suddenly remembered the words.

After leaving the temple she wandered down the pavement

alongside a busy road until she arrived at a weekend market. A fat middle-aged woman was unloading a pickup truck. She looked like a farmer who'd travelled from one of the provinces to sell her produce in Bangkok. Nid could hear her puffing away, and noticed her sweat-soaked shirt. As she walked past the truck, she saw a sack of chillies had burst open, with the contents spilled over the pavement. Without thinking, Nid bent down and began helping the chubby woman collect the chillies. Soon they'd put them all in a rattan basket.

"You're such a good girl," puffed the chubby woman, "will you stay with me a little longer? I could really do with a hand!" The pickup was loaded with durian, mangosteen, bamboo shoots, rambutan, dragon fruit and longan berries, as well as sacks of chillies. Nid helped carry the produce to a market stall about a dozen yards away. It took her almost an hour to unload everything, by which time her uniform was dirty and wrinkled. Seeing the state of her clothes, Nid flinched for a moment before she remembered that she'd left the orphanage and wouldn't be disciplined for it. The chubby woman noticed Nid's distress and smiled as she went over to her pickup, returning with a bundle of clothes.

"Here darling, I'll take your clothes to the laundry shop but you can wear these for now; they're my daughter's." Nid quickly changed into a pair of farmer's denim pants and a blouse, out of sight from the market traders and shoppers. She blended in immediately and got to work serving customers and dividing the chillies into small plastic bags. After the chubby lady got her some sticky rice with pork from one of the other stalls, Nid asked her for a job. The woman's face became sad. "I'm so sorry, I only sell in Bangkok at the weekend markets and my daughter usually comes with me, so I can't offer you a job. If you don't mind waiting a bit, I'll ask around as I know a lot of the vendors here." She returned almost an hour later, by which time it was evening. The laundry shop had already closed and Nid still had to find somewhere to sleep. "Stay with me until Sunday evening," said the woman. "You can work here this weekend and I'll give you 500 baht. Who knows what might turn up?" Nid slept with her in the cab of the pickup that Friday night and the rest of the weekend. She showered each morning and night at the back of the market where there were some basic showers and toilets. On the Sunday morning a vendor handed her a piece of paper ripped from a notice board that read:

JUNIOR ASSISTANT NEEDED TO RESTOCK SHELVES
AND KEEP THE STORE CLEAN AND ORGANIZED.
APPLY IN PERSON AT 7-ELEVEN STORE.

Nid politely asked the chubby woman if she could leave the market stall and then went to visit the 7-Eleven store a hundred yards away. "The manager isn't in," the girl at the cash register told her, "come back later just before the evening shift."

"What is the job exactly?" asked Nid.

The cashier pointed at the shelves and large fridges. "Just keeping them stocked and mopping the floors. It's easy – anyone can do it." The girl smiled, showing the metal wire of her braces. Nid returned to the market, but no longer felt interested in helping. The afternoon seemed to pass very slowly as she waited to go to the interview at the end of the day.

When Nid returned to the store, the cashier showed her braces through her smile again. "Just sit down here. The manager should be here any moment." As Nid waited she could see the store was understaffed – the floor was a little dirty and there were some empty spaces on the shelves.

"My name is Lek," said the cashier as Nid waited. Lek asked where Nid lived, and without thinking she mentioned the area beside the orphanage. "Oh, that is far – you'll spend hours in traffic. If you want, you can be my flatmate. I'm struggling with my rent and looking for someone to share," said Lek.

"But I don't have any money; I'll get 500 baht tonight but that's it," Nid replied.

Lek smiled again. "You'll get paid 1500 baht a week, and the rent isn't due until the end of the month. There's plenty of time to save up your half of the rent," she said reassuringly.

"Do you think I'll get the job?" asked Nid.

"I'll talk to the manager. I really need someone to help me with the rent."

While waiting patiently for the manager Nid suddenly had an urgent need to pee and asked were the toilet was. When she returned, a bald middle-aged Chinese man was operating the cash register. He had an expressionless face, and without saying a word he motioned for Nid to sit down. After he'd finished serving a customer he said, "This is a full-time job, but you'll also be asked to do overtime if needed. You'll keep this place spotless and stock the fridges and shelves. I want you to start tomorrow morning, but you need to pay for your own uniform."

"She can borrow one of mine," shouted Lek from behind a shelf. The manager returned to the cash register and Lek told Nid she'd meet her at the market after her shift. By the time Lek turned up at the market stall, most of the cabbages and other vegetables had been sold and Nid was loading the rest into the pickup. The chubby woman handed Nid a big plastic bag with unsold fruit and the promised 500 baht. Lek had been waiting and tried to kill the time by swiping on her smartphone. After Nid said her thanks and goodbyes to the chubby woman, they boarded a songthaew[1] and left for Lek's apartment.

---

1 A songthaew is a passenger vehicle adapted from a pick-up or a larger truck and used as a shared taxi or bus.

10

Nid

"What do you think?" Lek asked me as she showed me the basic studio room with a bed, a closet, a bathroom and a small sink out on the balcony. "Do you want to move in with me?"

I realized how Lek needed this arrangement as much as I did. "Yes, I like it," I said. And with that, the deal was done.

Only three days after leaving the orphanage I had 500 baht in my pocket, a roof over my head and a job. All my recent misfortunes now seemed like a distant memory after the events of the last few days. I settled into my new life with ease. I again wore a uniform, this time consisting of a green-lined blouse with a 7-Eleven logo on the top-left pocket, and black trousers. I still wore the black shoes from the orphanage. I didn't feel comfortable going outdoors either in my 7-Eleven uniform or my old orphanage clothes so I stayed in my room for the first week when not at work to avoid spending money until I could buy a long T-shirt style dress and flip flops.

My first wage seemed like a lot of money and it was certainly more than I'd ever had before. I tried saving as much as I could until my money filled an empty cigarette carton. When that was full I used my old student ID-card to open a bank account. I couldn't put in much to begin with as I still had to buy a uniform and needed to set aside five hundred baht each week to cover my half of the rent and utilities. My savings steadily increased, helped along by accepting all the overtime hours offered at the store. After a few months stocking shelves I was promoted to a sales clerk. I liked night shifts the most because in the small hours there were very few customers, and those that came into the store late at night were different from the daytime customers. Apart from party animals leaving clubs or bars, there were also taxi drivers coming in for energy drinks to stay awake and prostitutes buying condoms or K-Y Jelly and some snacks or liquor on their way home after finishing for the night. My new friend Lek spent the quiet hours chatting away on her smartphone, thinking that one day she would find a husband through it. She talked to a lot of foreigners through several chat apps and was always talking to foreigners in Europe and the US during their evenings. That seemed like a good idea to me, but I didn't have a smartphone. Lek helped me buy one at an electronics market for four thousand baht –

almost a month's salary. She also put some popular chat apps on the phone for me. The night shifts were different after that, and I played on my smartphone during the quiet hours of the night shifts. I found a translation app to help with my English and I chatted a lot with men, most of them twice my age. Nothing came of it, but it started me on what was to become a steep learning curve.

One night, I overheard a call girl talking on her mobile. The English-language lessons from the orphanage volunteers helped me to understand some of the conversation. The girl agreed to go to a foreigner's room, for which she demanded three thousand baht. She wore high heels and a skirt so short that it barely covered her backside, together with a blouse that exposed a lot of cleavage. I handed over her change and the girl smiled and left the shop, wiggling her curvy bum. The girl returned a few nights later to buy more condoms and K-Y Jelly. She laughed when I told her I'd never had a date.

"I've never had a boyfriend," I confessed. "I'm a bit scared."

"You're so lucky!" the call girl said. "I gave my virginity away for nothing because I was so stupid. Do you know that Japanese men pay a lot of money for a beautiful virgin girl? Why give it away for free for someone just to say 'thanks'?

I have a Japanese customer who would love to pay twenty thousand baht to pop your cherry."

I hesitated.

"Don't worry, the Japanese are like this," the call girl continued as she waved a little finger. "You won't feel a thing and it'll be over in five minutes, believe me I know. I'll come with you – you'll be fine."

I agreed and the girl promised to organize a double date with the Japanese guy. She said her name was Som, meaning orange, and we added each other on LINE, a chat app. I became restless thinking about the twenty thousand baht I was going to earn, and also about what I might have to do for it. I didn't have time to worry about it for long though as Som texted me the following day. The meet-up was going to be at midnight. Lek supportively offered to do my night shift at the store. Although her own search for a husband hadn't worked out, Lek watched my developments with great interest. I smiled gratefully but was too nervous to talk much.

Som called me that evening, and asked me to come down from my apartment as she was coming in a taxi.

"You don't need to dress up or wear any makeup. Our customer will take care of that," Som told me over the phone.

I got into the taxi in a T-shirt and flip flops. It took about an hour of sitting in heavy traffic to get to Thonglor district, a part of Bangkok I had never seen before. The area was full of huge condominium blocks, Japanese bars, restaurants and supermarkets.

Thonglor District, Bangkok

Bangkok's Thonglor district is home to about half of Thailand's Japanese residents. Bangkok has the fourth largest Japanese expatriate population of any city in the world outside Japan, behind only Los Angeles, New York City and Shanghai. The Japanese make up the largest expatriate group in Thailand and their purchasing power is huge, even for western standards as their expatriate salaries are based on the Japanese cost of living, one of the highest in the world.

Nid

Som directed the driver to a tall building that housed luxury high-end condos. The entrance was guarded by uniformed security staff who only granted access to the complex after confirmation from a resident. The two of us stood in silence as the lift took us up to the twentieth floor. Som calmly checked her messages on the way up, while I felt a knot in my stomach.

A door opened as we approached the condo entrance.

The Japanese man standing in the doorway was bald with a face that looked exactly like a toad. He bowed and said, "*Konbanwa.*" Despite his foreboding appearance, his submissive attitude allayed my fears somewhat. He led both of us into a dimly lit living room that offered an astonishing view of the Bangkok skyline. A teapot and wooden cups were neatly arranged on a low table at the centre of the room. The man ushered Som and me over to a sofa consisting of soft cushions before pouring hot *sake* from a teapot into wooden cups. He spoke with Som in English with a heavy accent that I couldn't understand. Som took me by the arm and guided me to a bedroom where a short black skirt, knee socks and a white blouse were laid out on the bed. On closer inspection I realized there was no underwear. Som instructed me to get into the somewhat childish costume while she changed into red lingerie that left her buttocks, vagina and nipples exposed.

When we returned to the living room we found the man drinking sake naked on the sofa. He beckoned us over and gestured for us to sit beside him while he stroked his erect penis. It was so small that Som was able to take both his penis and scrotum in her mouth. Her cheeks moved inwards while she sucked. After a while, the man pushed Som away as he didn't want to have an orgasm with her. He motioned for me to sit on the table. He kneeled in front of me and spread my legs open. He opened the lips of my vagina with two silver teaspoons.

He mumbled something admiringly as he tried to look inside my vagina, and then he inserted his tongue. I wanted to push him away, but the warning in Som's eyes stopped me just in time. I felt nothing but disgust as the Japanese guy ate me down there. He was so utterly unattractive and didn't even appear human. It was nothing like when Tukataa once kissed me down there in the orphanage. Som got on the floor to give the man another blowjob, but he spoke quickly in his accented English and she moved back to the sofa. Som told me to stand up while she got on her knees and inserted her tongue into my vagina, using the same teaspoons to open me. This time it was more pleasurable, but not so much that I would orgasm, especially not with such an ugly creature looking at me with his bulging eyes. It wasn't until later that I realized the man had instructed Som to prepare me for his entry.

The pleasant feeling of Som licking me was only temporary, and it disappeared entirely when the Japanese man kneeled behind me and started licking my anus. It felt weird and uncomfortable, and I disliked the fact that the creep was now behind me. As he licked, he reached up and squeezed my breasts. I knew he wanted to penetrate me soon. Som told me to lie on my back on the sofa and keep my legs wide open. The Japanese man mounted and penetrated me, but after just a minute he pulled out and orgasmed on my tummy. I didn't feel the penetration though, and only realized I'd lost my virginity when I saw drops of blood on the cushion. I expected it to be over at that point, but it wasn't. The Japanese man went down on me again, licking and swallowing the mixture of my blood and his semen.

The experience was gross, but the end was nearing. The Japanese man suggested Som and I shower, and after we'd finished and returned to the living room, he'd gone. We waited in silence until he returned wearing a bathrobe and carrying a silver-plated tray with two bundles of banknotes and two bottles of perfume. He bowed and said, "*Arigatogozaimashita*, please accept my gifts." It was clear that it was time for us to leave.

The following day I worked a double-shift to make up for the one Lek had covered the night before. I was on autopilot during both shifts, while the events of the previous night replayed over and over in my mind.

11

Tony

We walked to Nid's Toyota in the hotel parking lot and joined the heavy traffic. It took more than an hour to reach the highway leading out of Bangkok. The Impact Arena stadium is in Pak Kret district in Nonthaburi province, not far from Don Muang, Bangkok's old airport, which was visible from the elevated road. The stadium was huge, with thousands of spectators already seated when we arrived. Several matches were scheduled that evening but they seemed a bit too lame to watch. The main fight between a Thai and a Nigerian was unimpressive. The Thai was muscular but small, and he'd clearly received a lot of punches in the face during his career. His nose had been battered completely flat and resembled that of a boxer dog. The Nigerian he was facing off against was huge, so I put my money on him.

I couldn't have been more wrong. Although the Thai fighter's short stature meant that he took a lot of punches to his head and upper torso, he didn't seem bothered by them and the Nigerian eventually wore himself out. The fight was decided on mental alertness, courage and physical strength. When the Thai fighter got the upper hand he was ruthless and didn't let up his attacks until the Nigerian collapsed.

The public roared and shouted, "Ma Boxer!" I later learned that his name did actually mean "boxer dog". After the match we returned to the Toyota but the exit roads were clogged with cars and taxis. Hundreds of people were attempting to flag down taxis, but many decided to compromise and got into cramped minivans. Two cars ahead was a Mercedes, a recent model. The door opened and a girl got out, wearing high heels and a short skirt that showed her nylon stockings. She was clearly a hooker. She approached our car and knocked on the driver's window. When Nid rolled down the window I recognized the hooker as Yayee. They talked in Thai and I couldn't understand, but Nid explained that Yayee was with her Chinese customer and was inviting us for a few drinks at a nearby bar to wait for the traffic to ease. The Mercedes made a U-turn and we followed it until it stopped in a residential area in front of a local restaurant that had tables set up in a garden.

The Chinese man introduced himself as Bao Shen. He seemed a shy and introverted type, and when Yayee spoke Thai with him he just nodded. He said very little as we three talked, and he was scrutinizing something on his large smartphone. Yayee explained that he was an app developer. It wasn't until later I learned he was checking his earnings from this evening's match. I feel a bit scared of Bao Shen. The morning after we'd met him, Nid told me "I'm sure he's some sort of mafia figure."

I just laughed it off. "No," I said, "he's an app developer, Yayee explained it to me last night."

"Do you know what this app is for?" asked Nid. "It's related to gambling on Thai boxing, and the jails here are full of gamblers – it's illegal in Thailand!"

Nid packed her travel bag to get herself ready for her regular job, having already changed into her uniform. After she left, I thought it a good idea to try and get some information about the Chinese guy, and I used the hotel's internal phone system to call his room. Yayee answered the phone. "He's still asleep, but come over now and I'll make you some coffee," she said.

Yayee opened the door wearing a waitress uniform and guided me over to a huge dining table. "He likes a Chinese-style breakfast," she explained, pointing to the bowls she'd prepared for him that were filled with steamed buns stuffed with meat, noodles and chopped scallions, as well as pickled mustard and some other items I didn't recognize. She poured me a cup of hot coffee and it wasn't until I was on my second cup that the Chinese guy came out, unshaven and wearing a bathrobe. He clearly wasn't a happy early riser. After he'd slurped down his noodles, I handed over the file of photos of the boiler-room operator. He studied it with an expressionless face.

"Your friend?" he asked.

"No, just someone I have unfinished business with," I replied.

"I don't know this man," he said abruptly as he handed the file back to me. When I returned to my room I went through the file again and decided to stake out the boiler-room office building the next day.

I found a coffee shop opposite the office entrance. The place was occupied by Thais and foreigners focused on their laptops, tablets and smartphones. Without a device I didn't blend in very well, so I made a mental note to bring one with me the next time. I figured I could even record anyone of interest with a webcam if needed. Through the corporate investigator I knew the boiler room was on the top floor, but it seemed impossible to distinguish between the boiler-room employees and the other office workers. I had to find a way of figuring who the boiler-room staff were and decided to return the next day.

Bao Shen

As soon as the American left I phoned my uncle to tell him what had happened. He listened and told me to find out more details. I thought that Yayee might have more information so I sat her down to talk. She explained that the American wasn't one of her customers, but she'd managed to get some money out of him by humiliating a farang in Pattaya. I smiled when she told me how much he'd paid for it. Tony wasn't just another sex tourist, he was here for another purpose. I couldn't quite wrap my head around him, but his inquiries about my competition and the money he gave to Yayee just to humiliate another farang piqued my interest.

Yayee

Although I didn't understand much Chinese, I understood that Bao Shen was talking to someone about Tony. Bao Shen bowed several times, even though only speaking on the phone. I realized the other person must be very important and wondered what the conversation was about. It seemed that

Bao Shen hadn't been entirely truthful with Tony when he denied knowing the person in the photo. Bao Shen then sat me down and asked me lots of questions about Tony. This made me even more confused and uncomfortable as I didn't want to be in a position where I had to favour one over the other.

Tony

I'd been hanging around the coffee shop for several days. I'd observed that the boiler room had two crews who operated in separate shifts – most likely due to the time difference between Bangkok and the United States. This helped me separate the normal office workers who all ended their working day at around 5 or 6 pm from the boiler-room staff who arrived and finished during the shift change later in the day. Almost every evening I saw a young Caucasian guy wearing a sun cap and with bad acne scars on his face entering the building. He always came in at around 8 pm and never left before 2 am. One evening I watched him as he spoke to another westerner. When the older westerner pointed a finger in his face the young guy didn't react and looked uncomfortable. On closer inspection I recognized the older one – he was the man in the photos that the corporate investigator had given me. It was Hubert, the owner and operator of the boiler room.

12

Bao Shen

My uncle made some inquiries with relatives in the United States about the American. We Chinese are everywhere, you know, and if we don't know someone in a particular country, a friend or a friend-of-a-friend will. Some unknown person in the United States punched in the name and passport number that Yayee had acquired from the check-in counter. Through that my uncle found Tony's social-security number, which in turn gave my uncle access to a lot more data. I received an emailed dossier on the American. He turned out to be a military officer who'd been in the army for over twenty years and had been discharged quite recently. It didn't seem likely that an officer honourably discharged only a short time ago could be part of the gang that had copied my app and stolen my customers. My curiosity got the upper hand. I asked Yayee to invite the American up for a drink and another talk. This time I told Yayee not to wear the short-skirted waitress uniform, since

Yayee had made it clear that this wasn't to Tony's taste as he was only into real girls. I ordered baked potatoes, meatloaf and a mixture of lettuce, bell peppers, carrots and broccoli from the kitchen downstairs. Not my favourite food, but I'd seen Americans order it and assumed Yayee's friend would like it. To be honest, I don't generally feel comfortable with westerners. When I first met Tony after the boxing match we didn't exactly hit it off. He must have felt the same when he entered the apartment since he had a somewhat puzzled look on his face. I think we both forced ourselves to be polite, but both relaxed a bit during the small talk over dinner.

"My uncle found out about the man you inquired after," I said. "He's my competitor and is also active in online sports gambling. I don't think I like him. He isn't playing a fair game." I wanted to test Tony's response to determine whether he was in some way connected with my rival app operator.

"You might not like him," replied Tony, "which is probably all right for you, but I have stronger feelings. I hate the guy. I want to find out what he's up to and I'll try to hurt him where it hurts the most."

Tony then told me about what had happened, right from when he'd found his dead father through to meeting me that evening. It was a long story, and almost an hour passed before he'd finished.

Finally, I asked, "How are you going to get your revenge?"

"I have no plan for now," said Tony. "I'm gathering as much information as I can and I'll see what I can do with it."

I nodded and thought it over for a while before finally offering my hand. "The enemies of my enemies are my friends. I'm not sure if I can be of any help, but I certainly will help if I can."

Tony

When I entered Frank Reitz's office I found the corporate investigator at his desk.

"Take a seat," said Frank as he opened some files on his computer. "I have something for you. The westerner you saw is called Donald. He's a language student from New Zealand, although he assumes that role just to obtain a student visa. He probably doesn't even go to any classes but just pays the tuition fee to maintain and renew his visa. Working on this type of visa is strictly prohibited, but the kind of money these guys earn makes it is easy for them to buy their way out of any problems. Besides, this Donald seems like the number-two guy. You should focus on Hubert the boiler-room owner. If you want, I can get my private investigator to find out where he lives. You won't get away with doing that yourself though, he'll spot a westerner on his tail."

I nodded, understanding my conspicuousness.

"Okay," said Frank. "Just be patient and wait for my update."

Nothing much happened over the following days while I waited for Frank's call. I spent a lot of the time in the rooftop pool, I cleared a backlog of emails and spent a few nights and afternoons with Nid when she wasn't working at the convenience store. The call came on Monday morning, the following week.

"Let me email it to you," said Frank. "I have recent pictures of Hubert and his residence."

I scrutinized the pictures that arrived in my inbox and decided to have a look at the residential building where Hubert was living. Frank informed me that he was on the sixteenth floor.

Speaking to the bored-looking girl at reception, I pretended to be interested in renting an apartment. "Can you show me some units, please?" I asked. She smiled and called someone. A second girl appeared who seemed to be a copy of the first. She also smiled and asked me to follow her to a small meeting room beside the main lobby. She then presented me with a brochure that included a floor plan and a price list.

The place was a fairly upscale and made up of serviced apartments going for the equivalent of $5,000 per month for a fifteen hundred square foot condo. The rent included housekeeping, maintenance and cleaning on a daily or weekly basis, depending on the contract. I asked if there were any units available on the fifteenth, sixteenth or seventeenth floors. She typed on her keyboard and said yes, there were a few units available on those floors.

After disappearing somewhere for a short while she returned carrying a keyring with labelled room keys. We took the lift, which had a security camera inside, up to the sixteenth floor. Walking out into the lift landing on that floor, I saw several more security cameras that observed the whole floor, including the front doors of the condo units. I imagined that somewhere in the building a security guard was sitting in front of multiple monitors.

Just over halfway down the landing I spotted the condo number that Frank had emailed to me. I was taken to view a condo unit that was two doors away from it. After the sales girl showed me the unit I inquired whether there was a better view from the seventeenth floor. I made a mental note as we passed by Hubert's room. I thought I should try to get a unit as close to Hubert's as possible on the floor above. Like the sixteenth floor, the seventeenth was also littered with security cameras throughout the landing. None of the two available units on the seventeenth floor were directly above Hubert's though, so I also asked to see what was available on the fifteenth floor. The one directly below Hubert's was available and I liked it even before the girl had unlocked the door. This unit, which was decorated in an Art Deco style, contained a living room, kitchen and two bedrooms. The girl explained that the minimum rental period was three months, and I'd need to pay a one-month deposit and month's rent in advance. When we got back to her office I signed the lease and handed over my AMEX card. The $10,000 charge worried me a little as I wasn't used to spending that kind of money. Anyway, it was done and I pushed my financial doubts to the back of my mind. It was Friday and I planned to move in on the Monday morning. Once I'd returned to my current living quarters in Thonglor I gave the office notice that I'd be moving out.

13

Nid

A farang guy had been messaging me on Tinder. He couldn't host me in his home and wanted to have sex in a love hotel. I guessed that he was likely a married expat who'd been sent to Bangkok with his family by an American or European company. It was an easy gig and I could do it after my evening shift at 7-Eleven. The guy was waiting for me in a coffee shop, and he paid up as soon as I arrived. We got into a taxi and he gave the taxi driver directions in reasonable Thai, which confirmed my guess that he was an expat who'd been here for a while already.

There are many five-star-style love hotels in Bangkok that usually have large flat-screen TVs for watching porn or playing music. They normally have an indoor Jacuzzi, and some even have an outdoor Jacuzzi or a private pool, although the ones in this district are not generally frequented by farangs. Farangs instead tend to use love hotels – better known as short-time hotels – mainly in the Silom and Sukhumvit areas. The rooms in these short-time hotels are often so shabby that the carpets have partially disintegrated, while the furniture can be described as "authentic vintage". This love hotel was no different. A sealed plastic bag lay on the bed, containing two clean but well-worn towels and two bars of cheap soap. The farang didn't seem to mind and he enthusiastically got down to business as soon as we'd showered. He was like Lucky Luke and fired minutes after getting his gun into position. I got fifteen hundred baht for it. Not bad for an assistant at 7-Eleven, huh? I spent only half an hour with him, including the time for the 'before and after' showers.

After showering I called the front desk to order a taxi. I was going to meet Yayee for some street food at a place near my home, but my heart suddenly stopped as I left the room. I froze and felt as if I'd been struck by a bolt of lightning. Breathless, I grabbed a door handle to stop myself from fainting. Further down the hallway, a skinny girl was leaving one of the rooms accompanied by a fat Indian. When I finally gasped for air she recognized me and ran over. We didn't say anything but just grabbed hold of each other and then hugged and kissed. Tukataa touched my face and said "Hi, Nid" and we both broke down and cried like babies. The farang and the Indian just stood there for a while, clearly feeling uncomfortable and unsure what to do. When we just ignored them they both eventually left. I pulled Tukataa back into the room and we sat down on the bed holding each other's hands. We both began talking at the same time; there was so much to say.

I don't know how long we'd spoken for when Yayee called telling me to hurry up since she was already at the food stall. When I told her what had happened, she ordered takeaway somtam pokpok with kunio, my favourite dish. She also bought a bottle of Sangsom rum and some Coke before hopping in a taxi to meet us. Tukataa and I were still chatting and holding hands when Yayee knocked on the door. She placed the food on the small table and filled three glasses with Sangsom, Coke and ice. Reception called and told us that our time was up, but Yayee went downstairs and paid for the room until the following morning. That night we all laughed, cried and got drunk. I think it was the happiest night of my life.

Bao Shen

Yayee returned early the next morning. I suspected she'd been a slut and had sucked some farang cock somewhere, which is all right since I'm not into boring good girls. I prefer my girls to have a dick and they must be kinky and dirty. But she explained that she hadn't been with any guys and told me how Nid had been reunited with someone close from her past. I wasn't that interested to be honest, but I *was* interested when she told me she'd met Tony downstairs in the lobby and he was moving to a condo in another district. Tony was apparently moving into the same building where our person of mutual interest was living. He was clearly up to something.

"Tony asked me to tell you," said Yayee, "he wants to talk to you before he moves over there." A little later I took the lift down a few floors and knocked on the American's door. He opened it himself and beckoned me inside. He was in the middle of packing, ready to move to his new place, and it looked like he was almost finished.

"We should be allies, we both want to hurt him," suggested Tony as he showed me a screenshot on his smartphone – it was a list of WiFi networks. "I took this screenshot at my new place. One of these networks belongs to him. Do you see any chance of finding out which one is his and then hacking into it so I can monitor what he's doing online?"

"That's easy," I replied, "but not for me. I'm an app developer not a hacker. I know the perfect person for this job though. I'll message her."

Tony

I had to tell Nid to lay off for a while since she didn't really fit into my new environment. I told her I was occupied with business, which strictly speaking wasn't too far from the truth. I didn't want to do anything until Bao Shent the hacker over to my new place. Meanwhile, I decided to pursue the second-in-command of the boiler-room operation. Frank's file included his address and photo, and I'd personally seen the guy outside the office building while staking it out, so I knew I'd recognize him.

This Donald guy lived in an apartment building much less fancy than his boss's condo. With no shops or restaurants facing the building from where I could observe, I settled for a small lunchroom nearby that also served drinks. I couldn't even see the entrance to Donald's building from there, but it was the only place where I could pass a bit of time without attracting any attention. As it turned out, Donald came here for lunch before leaving for the office. I'd just ordered my food when he barged in and shouted his order to the staff, before sitting down and immediately pulling out his smartphone to begin working on it. I glanced over his shoulder, pretending to be on my way to the toilet. He appeared to be swiping on some sort of dating app. I couldn't recognize which app it was but saw him swiping through a ladyboy's profile. It was certainly not a vanilla-dating app as the images were explicit hardcore pictures – not the type of photos that would make a straight guy horny.

Moments later my mobile rang; it was Bao Shen wanting to visit me at my new place. I paid up and hailed a taxi. The front desk called from downstairs just as I walked through the door of my new home. Bao Shen had arrived and was on his way up. He hauled in a suitcase and set it in the middle of the living room. When he opened it I saw there was something that looked like a router inside. "It's a Kracker," he explained.

KRACK attack

A KRACK attack is a method were the "handshake" between a WiFi network and a device is registered and recorded when the device attempts to login into a WiFi network. The device and the network usually share an encryption key for future traffic, meaning that a device will be able to read data once it has that key. Hackers abuse this process by copying a key that's already in use in order to decrypt and read all messages sent over the network.

Tony

Bao Shen hooked up the Kracker to my WiFi network. "It'll send the data it collects to someone in China," he told me. "She'll gain access to whichever files you need from your neighbour. We can then have a peek at those files."

"Will this definitely work?" I asked.

"It normally does," answered Bao Shen, "but there are no guarantees. You couldn't use this technique to hack a bank or government office, but apart from that it usually works."

I told him I'd traced Donald to his apartment and had managed to get a glimpse of his smartphone screen in a nearby lunchroom. Of course, I knew Bao Shen was into ladyboys, so somewhat reluctantly, I told him about the ladyboy porn I saw on Donald's smartphone.

He laughed, "Donald will like Yayee! She liked that job you gave her in Pattaya, and I'm sure she'll be happy to do another for you."

After hesitating briefly I said, "Let's see what comes out of the Kracker first." That evening I dined in a local restaurant not far from my new place. It was nothing fancy, but there was a small garden beside it where I had coffee and a cigar before deciding to leave early. My new residence had a gym and I wanted to work out first thing the next morning. That plan didn't materialize though, as a few moments after going through the door of my condo the phone rang.

It was Bao Shen again. "I have some bad news." I listened while he talked. "We could hack into every WiFi network on your floor. The network you are after is heavily encrypted. We can see a lot of data being transferred in and out, but we don't know where it's going to or coming from. His connection and data are so heavily encrypted that you can only access it if you're looking over his shoulder." We spoke a little more about other possibilities, but got nowhere.

I couldn't sleep that night and just kept turning over. I only managed to fall into a light sleep in the early morning. By that time I'd forgotten all about my plan to do a workout. Later that morning I received a phone call from reception saying that a visitor was waiting for me. Wondering who it was, I took the lift down. Yayee was waiting in the lobby, and as usual she was swiping on her smartphone. She looked up as I got closer and noticed the surprised look on my face.

"Bao Shent me," she said, "I have to do another job for you."

"What could that be?" I asked. I was a bit annoyed to be confronted with something I didn't know about, but Yayee explained what Bao Shen wanted her to do and my mood improved a bit.

"Okay," I told her. "Come up and I'll give you what you need. I have the name and address of the restaurant somewhere."

Yayee

It was after midnight but the restaurant was crowded. Donald had presumably just closed the office and was having another meal before going home. We knew he often came here for something to eat after work. He had managed to get a table to himself in the far corner of the restaurant and was digging through a plate of what looked like chicken fried rice and he was nursing a bottle of Chang beer.

"May I?" I said, keeping my voice low and manly.

Donald looked up and saw a gorgeous ladyboy before him. I was dressed in a short skirt and was showing a lot of cleavage, and I was carrying a plate of food. I pretended to be searching for a seat and looked at Donald with a raised eyebrow, and when he failed to respond immediately I leant forward both to place my plate on his table and offer the lucky boy a good look down my blouse. He didn't fail to notice my amazing boobs and I could see he was becoming horny.

"*Kob khun ka*," I said as I planted my ass in the seat. I

made small talk as we ate, and told the farang that I owned a hair salon that also offered pedicures and skin treatments.

"Where do you live?" he asked me.

I told him I had a unit in a condo block in an upmarket district of Bangkok, which happened to be close to where his boss lived. I caught Donald glancing at my cleavage as I knew he would.

"What brings you to Bangkok?" I asked.

"I'm the manager of an investment firm," the boy replied, exaggerating and unable to take his eyes off my boobs.

"Oooh," I said, "I couldn't be your client as I've just bought a new condo and I've spent all my money!"

"You bought a condo in that building?" he asked.

"Yeah, do you wanna see my new place? I've just moved in but there are a few beers in the fridge."

A little later and we were both sitting in the back of a taxi. We didn't speak but I lightly caressed Donald's knee. I knew he was preparing for an unforgettable evening. The taxi dropped us off at the entrance of the condo building. It was like most other condos in Bangkok; a security guard sat at the entrance to the car park, and another was stationed at the reception desk. The lifts could only be operated using a keycard. Bao Shen had rented the place for two nights, just in case one night wasn't enough for our needs. Donald of course had no idea that he was walking into a place that was rented temporarily, and genuinely believed that I was a rich businesswoman. And why not. I poured him a beer and told him I'd change into something more comfortable.

"Please help me unzip," I said, and turned my curvy ass towards him. As he fumbled with the zipper, I reached behind and stroked his cock. "Hurry up, babe," I said, "we need to take a shower and then I want you to eat me." My dress fell, revealing my lack of underwear, leaving me in high heels and stockings and nothing else. Donald took a final glance at his phone on the sofa before I pulled him into the bathroom.

Bao Shen had been waiting in the spare room, and as soon as we disappeared into the bathroom, he entered the living room. He first took photos of the phone on the sofa to ensure he could position it exactly as Donald had left it. He then plugged it into his laptop and created a hidden folder in the smartphone's operating system before starting to transfer spyware into the new folder. He'd acquired the spyware from a dark-web site and had made a few modifications for this purpose. He returned Donald's smartphone on the sofa exactly as he'd found it, and quietly left the condo. As he went down in the lift he phoned me.

"My mum!" I exclaimed after ending the call. "I have to see her immediately – she isn't well." I hurriedly got dressed and asked Donald to pull up my zipper. This time he handled it with much less pleasure. "Please see yourself out," I said as I went to leave. "I'll call you."

Poor Donald must have wondered how I could call him since we hadn't exchanged numbers.

Bao Shen was laughing when I arrived at his condo. As he closed his laptop he said, "And now tell me what you were doing to that guy when I called you? Have you been a naughty slut?"

14

Tony

I woke up and changed into a sweat suit with the intention of finally making it to the gym but just before I'd gone out the door I got a call from downstairs. The Chinese guy was waiting for me in the lobby. He was carrying a laptop case and informed me he'd managed to gain access to Donald's smartphone and wanted to install some monitoring software on my computer. "This is how it works," he began as we sat down at my dining table. My laptop screen displayed a dashboard menu for every function of Donald's smartphone. "Text messages and emails are automatically displayed here," Bao Shen explained. "You can open them just by clicking the icons displayed here. There are some extra functions, too. All the calls he makes or receives will be recorded and forwarded to you when the smartphone is not in use and is connected to WiFi. I've set it up to send you the recordings at 3 am – hopefully he'll be sleeping then. Another function integrated in this spyware will also allow you to activate the smartphone's microphone to record his offline conversations. This might not always work very well because it's sensitive to background noise. So long as he isn't in a nightclub or walking on a busy street it should work well enough though. However, if you find out that Donald will have a meeting at a certain time, you can pre-set the system to record the audio for a specific length of time."

"Will Donald find out that his phone has been tampered with?" I asked.

"Not a chance," Bao Shen stated confidently. "These spy applications are hidden deep in the operating system and won't show up in the smartphone menu. Just remember to only download the recordings at night, and when the device is connected to WiFi. This will ensure he doesn't notice his smartphone slowing down a bit or showing the increased data usage or a drop the connection speed."

Pegasus spyware

NSO Group is an Israeli cyber-arms company which developed spyware that can be installed on smartphones running certain versions of iOS and most likely also Android. It became known as Pegasus spyware after it was discovered following a failed attempt to install it on an iPhone belonging to a human-rights activist. An investigation was launched and soon details were published about its abilities, and the security vulnerabilities it exploited. Pegasus spyware is capable of reading text messages, tracking calls, collecting passwords, tracing a smartphone's location, and gathering information from apps used on that smartphone. Apple later released a software update to block Pegasus. When Pegasus was first discovered it got a lot of media attention and at the time it was called the most sophisticated smartphone attack ever; it was the first time in iPhone history that a remote jailbreak exploit had been discovered. NSO Group stated that it only provides "authorized governments with technology to assist them in combat terror and crime".

Nid

As Tukataa had no place of her own, she spent her nights either staying with customers or sleeping rough. She wore a wrinkled dress and her hair was uncombed. I loved her as a sister, and I wasn't going to leave her on her own, so I told her to come and stay with me. That immediately created a problem though because Som didn't like the idea of Tukataa moving in with us. Without any hesitation, I decided to rent another place in the same building. Luckily, I was able to arrange it that day, and moved in immediately with Tukataa. "I want you to stay with me forever," I told her as we sat on the bed in our simple apartment. I went to the supermarket to buy her some toiletries, and picked up a few pots and pans in case she wanted to cook, as well as a small TV to keep her occupied. We spent most of our time sitting together in the room talking and watching TV, leaving the place only to buy street food or go shopping in the market. After a few days of this new routine I realized I couldn't keep ignoring the messages that were building up from my customers, especially because I'd quit my job at 7-Eleven and now had a "sister" to support. I met my customers in the evening or at night, and slept during the day while Tukataa was watching Thai soaps. Sometimes we spent time in the nearby shopping mall. I was very happy with this routine as I'd always felt so alone since Mum died, but all that had changed now. I could imagine living with Tukataa forever, and began to plan renting a house with a small garden. I had a few regular customers and business was good.

It wasn't quite so simple for Tukataa though. She soon became restless. She had a life of abuse and drug use behind her after all. Despite the improvement in her quality of life since she'd been living with me, I guess Tukataa gradually grew bored with this new life. To begin with, she would go out to buy yabaa only occasionally while I was with customers, but it soon became a regular part of her daily routine. I became suspicious when Tukataa began returning home late, but ignored these feelings as I didn't want Tukataa to feel uncomfortable. However, when I found yabaa tablets in the bathroom, I could no longer hide my concern, and I broke down one day. Tukataa tried to comfort me. She hugged me as she cried, promising never to take yabaa again. She flushed the tablets down the toilet, although I knew it was only for show. She was already an addict who could not control her cravings, and it was easy for her to obtain a regular supply of the drug. Tukataa began staying away from home at night more often until eventually she fell back into her previous lifestyle of living rough. It happened so gradually that I only really woke up to what had been happening after Tukataa disappeared completely. I was desperately sad and lonely.

Soon after, I received a message from John, a British guy who'd booked me for a night a year ago. He liked me and had continued messaging me after he'd returned home. Now he wanted to have a girlfriend experience and was offering me twenty thousand baht to travel around Thailand with him during his two-week holiday. I never get emotionally involved with customers, but the opportunity to forget the current situation – even if only for a short time – was appealing. So there I was, a week later, with a packed bag at Suvarnabhumi Airport awaiting a British Airways flight carrying the man who was to be my 'boyfriend' for the next two weeks.

The girlfriend experience

A girlfriend experience (GFE) is an arrangement between a sex worker and her client where they agree to blur the boundaries between a financial transaction and a romantic relationship particularly in which a client pays a prostitute to pretend to be his girlfriend. In this situation the sex worker provides not only sex but also some degree of emotional intimacy, which results in a more comprehensive experience for the client. While the details vary the idea is to include a sense of authenticity thus to make the experience more pleasurable for the client and of course to make the encounter, which can last days or weeks, more lucrative for the sex worker.

Yayee

I returned to Pattaya after the Chinese guy sent me away. It always happens, one way or another; they either run out of money, return home or get bored and move on to the next girl. I was used to it anyway, and went back to hanging around the streets and bars in Pattaya. It didn't take long before I got used to street life again. I returned to hooking, stealing and robbing, and it took me only a couple of days to get right back in the game. A few days after settling back in I went to a roadside stall selling Isaan food on a smaller soi connected to Beach Road. Although it was late afternoon, the sex workers were already out and about. Many of them went there because they liked to eat the local dishes their mum would cook for them at home. Luckily, I was able to find a free plastic stool on the pavement next to the food stall. I ordered *pad krapow*, a dish of stir-fried meat and vegetables with basil served with rice and a fried egg. As I was finishing the food, a girl grabbed me from behind and shouted, "*Aroi mai* [is it delicious]?" She held her hands over my eyes and said, "If you don't guess who I am, you'll have to buy me a plate of *pad krapow*!" I forced her hands away and turned around to see a girl with a wrinkled short dress and uncombed hair. "Hi, Yayee," said Tukataa before hugging me. She looked exactly the same street girl I remembered seeing the last time when we crossed paths in the Bangkok love hotel where she was with Nid. From the way she attacked her plate of rice, I gathered that she hadn't eaten for quite a while. She seemed genuinely happy to see me. As she gobbled down her food, she reminded me of my sister Nok back in Udon Thani. It was impossible not to like her. She talked non-stop as she ate. "Farang no good," she said as she chewed some meat. "Want dirty sex for little money. Making money not easy today." I called Nid to tell her about Tukataa, but Nid told me that some British guy had hired her for a few weeks while he travelled around southern Thailand. I decided to introduce Tukataa to a friend of mine, a mamasan in a bar on Soi 6.[2] The girls were allowed to stay there overnight in the short-time rooms upstairs, which I thought would at least give her a roof over her head.

Tony

The software Bao Shen had installed on my computer worked really well. It allowed me to read every email and text message that Donald sent and received, and I could also listen to his recorded mobile calls. It even allowed me to hear what he was watching on TV. It turned out that Donald wasn't as important to the organization as I'd thought though. He was really just an office manager. All the emails I'd scrutinized were merely related to administrative and staff-management arrangements, while his chat messages were largely with ladyboys. He was apparently just a foot soldier. What I really needed was to get the spyware installed on Hubert's hone. I called Bao Shen to

---

2 In Thailand and the Philippines the term mamasan is commonly used to describe a woman who manages female workers in bars and brothels.

ask if he could repeat the same game that he and Yayee had played with Donald.

"Is he into ladyboys?" asked Bao Shen, "and do you know where he hangs out?" I had to admit that I didn't have the slightest idea. The guy was living just one floor above me, but I'd only seen him in the lift where we'd exchanged a "Good morning" or a "Good evening" and nothing more. "I need his smartphone for a minute or two," Bao Shen said. "It doesn't matter where or when."

I phoned Frank Reitz and explained what I needed.

"What you want is almost impossible," Frank said. "Sure, I can figure out his daily routine, but who separates themselves from their phones these days? My phone spends more time with me than my wife! People take their phones to the toilet and into the bedroom. To be honest, I can't think of a situation where someone would separate themselves from their smartphone."

"Let's see what you can come up with," I said.

The Gentlemen's Club was tucked away at the end of a small soi. There was no outside sign to identify it, and no name was displayed on the building. The club had no website and was members only – membership was available only by introduction and for an annual fee of about one million baht. Non-members were admitted only when invited by a full member. The club took up all five floors of the building, and offered a Turkish bath, a sauna and a steam room. The bar, on the top floor, was well-stocked with imported beers and spirits. Beside it was a separate smoking room where Cuban and other high-quality imported cigars were stored in a humidor. Attractive girls who spoke excellent English, a handful of whom could also speak Japanese, were available as companions while members enjoyed a drink or cigar. The girls could be taken to one of the private rooms on the floor below. Evidently Hubert was a regular there, and had been a member for a long time. According to Frank, he normally came to the club every Tuesday and Thursday evening, and would spend some time in the steam room before going to the bar upstairs. Then he would usually take one of the available girls to a private room downstairs. Adjacent to the steam room was a locker room where members could store their car keys, phones and any other electronic equipment that would be vulnerable to the humidity of the steam room. Since it was a members-only club and the members placed a high value on their privacy, there were no security cameras around.

"Well," said Frank as he nursed his drink, "your best bet is the locker room. I managed to get an invitation through one of my clients and was able to get inside. The lockers have electronic keypads so someone will need to glance over Hubert's shoulder as he punches in his code. I'm certain his smartphone will be in there as it can't be taken into the steam room."

"One million baht to buy a membership?" I asked.

"Yes, and you'd also need to be introduced by a member," replied Frank.

15

Uncle Zheng

My nephew Bao Shen has always been a big nuisance. When my brother was on his deathbed, he made me promise to look after his son. I've had trouble with him ever since. I was glad to finally see him beginning to contribute to the family business through his Thai-boxing gambling operation, but now here he was phoning me asking for a million baht to buy a membership to some club.

I get sick and tired of this boy – there's no way that the family will agree to fund his perverted ventures. You know, he even had a *katoi* in his Bangkok condo, and I had to tell him to get rid of her. I'm so glad my brother is not around to see what his son has become. Bao Shen explained to me the details of his financial request, so I phoned a relative in Bangkok who arranged an invitation for a one-off visit to the club. I'm not sure it will do any good though; this boy only spells trouble. He had something good going with this gambling project, but now he' seems to have let it slip through his fingers.

Bao Shen

That was a piece of cake. The gweilo took no notice of me in the locker room and was oblivious to the fact I was reading the access code on his locker using mirrored lenses in my glasses when he opened it. As soon as the gweilo left for the steam room I opened his locker again. I connected Hubert's smartphone to my own with a cable and it took less than two minutes to upload and install the spyware. Once the installation was complete I took Hubert's keyless fob for his Mercedes. Using another app, it took about two minutes more for me to record the serial number and the frequency the fob used to communicate with the car's transponder. I replaced the smartphone and the fob as I'd found them and I closed the locker before joining the gweilo in the steam room. The gweilo was bragging to some other foreigners about the new Mercedes that he'd just bought.

"They're the safest cars in the world," he said.

We'll see about that, I thought.

Tony

Now I had two mobiles to monitor. I opened two separate

windows of the monitoring programme on my laptop and spent days listening to Hubert's conversations. I also had the microphone switched on most of the time when he wasn't on a call. He seemed to spend a lot of time in his apartment. I could see when he logged into his Hong Kong bank account, since each time he logged in he was sent an access code by SMS. Every time he logged in he would pound away at his keyboard, and I could only wish that I was able to look over his shoulder. He sent emails to Donald on a daily basis, but these were only office related. Meanwhile, the conversations I eavesdropped on were not incriminating. After a week I became a little disillusioned, since other than listening in to social calls I could only determine when he was doing internet banking or communicating with Donald. I began to doubt whether I'd be able to recover the funds stolen from my father or from Maura's clients. Meanwhile my bank balance was falling at an alarming pace. I called Bao Shen and said I didn't think our cooperation was going to bear any fruit.

"It's a shame about the money," Bao Shen replied, "but we can make him suffer all the same. And if we take him out, he can't continue."

Yayee

After leaving Tukataa in the care of my mamasan friend on Soi 6, I became quite busy as I managed to pick up a few customers. I also went to some boxing matches in Chonburi province only to see my old boxer friend Ma getting the shit kicked out of him. He was clearly having a bad run and it looked like his boxing career wasn't going to last much longer. I barely had time to think about it though because I received an alarming LINE message from my mamasan friend. A sex tourist had gotten rough with Tukataa and had beaten her. I couldn't find Tukataa when I arrived at the bar. The mamasan saw me looking around for her and told me that both her eyes were swollen and her face was bruised. She had been taken to the government hospital. On examining her, the medical staff there had apparently discovered that she also had two broken ribs.

"I had no idea ..." the mamasan told me. "Last night an obese farang bar-fined Tukataa to go back to his place."

"Where is that man?" I demanded.

The mamasan tried to dodge the blame, "He bar-fined another girl last night too, but he paid in full and she didn't have any problems."

"Where is she?" I repeated.

The mamasan called out for another girl to come over to give me the apartment address and unit number. I set off immediately. I felt the same rage pulsating through my veins that I experienced when my sister Nok had been attacked and raped.

The events that followed came back to me slowly over time. I remember a man at the front desk nodding to me as I entered, no doubt thinking to himself that someone had ordered another girl for the night. The fat farang was evidently already naked when I arrived, and must have been peering through the peephole in the door expecting his next hooker when he saw me, big breasted, long black hair shaping my face – how could he resist?

He made the decision to open the door to me and as soon as he did that I head-butted him in the chest. It had little effect on him though, his body fat absorbed the impact. He stepped back and as I tried to punch him he grabbed my hair and began pulling violently as he repeatedly punched me with his free fist. I fell onto the floor and he started kicking me. He landed the sole of his fake Timberland shoes a few times in my face, which broke my nose and crushed my cheek bones and an eye socket. I was enraged. I kicked upwards, first with little effect, but I finally managed to land a kick that made my long stiletto heel disappear into the fatso's crotch. He collapsed onto the floor and screamed in pain, but still managed to keep his grip on my hair. I remember biting one of his nipples with all my strength. The farang must have let go of my hair because I hit him with a half-empty beer bottle I had grabbed from a table. Then I was jumping on him in my stilettos. I lost a heel and it was sticking out of his belly. I had to kick my shoes off. The farang tried to crawl to the door so I jumped on his back and tried to insert the bottle into his asshole. I shoved the neck of the bottle in, put on my heelless shoe and stamped on the bottom of the bottle until it disappeared into his anus. I tried to break the bottle inside him by jumping on him but he was a human trampoline. When he made for the door again I kicked it closed, bashing his head and knocking him unconscious. I slowly dragged him back into the room and towards the balcony but I couldn't lift him over the rail, he was that fat. I was drained by this point. Finally I managed to lift his upper body onto the balcony railing and then haul up one leg. Once I'd lifted his leg high enough, his centre of mass shifted and his torso pulled the rest of him over the rail and down onto the car park below.

I noticed the group of neighbours had formed in front of the apartment door, wondering what the noise was all about. I walked towards them, blood streaming out of my crushed eye socket and nose, my shirt soaked with blood. The neighbours stepped back in horror. I staggered over to the lift and as the doors closed, I must have fainted. I later learnt that the residents called the emergency services, and they transported me to the Chonburi public hospital where I slipped into a coma. Apparently the police showed up in the hospital to interrogate me, but the doctor informed them I was suffering from severe concussion and it was uncertain I would ever wake up. The police ordered the doctor on duty to report any improvement in my condition and there I stayed.

Jennifer

Uncle Zheng told Bao Shen to send him all the files they'd stolen from the gweilo, including all the emails, recordings and any other data they'd collected. Uncle Zheng then had it copied to a memory card and asked for a favour from another family. Their business was harvesting online usernames and passwords, usually from the customers of banks and other financial institutions. They sent over one of their best: me.

"I'm retired," I told Uncle Zheng, "but my family has asked me to help you."

Uncle Zheng knew my age and my reputation. "How can

a twenty-four-year-old be retired?" he inquired.

I only smiled in response, since I was unwilling to explain to him how I'd made my fortune and many of the crimes I'd participated in remained unsolved. Some foot soldiers may have been arrested, but the masterminds had never even been identified. One of my proudest achievements was the Bangladesh Bank job.

The Bangladesh Bank cyber heist took place in February 2016, when instructions to fraudulently withdraw $1 billion from the account of the central bank of Bangladesh was issued via the SWIFT network. We made five transactions worth $101 million, which we withdrew from a Bangladesh Bank account at the Federal Reserve Bank of New York. The authorities traced $20 million to Sri Lanka and recovered that and they traced another $81 million to the Philippines but only recovered about $18 million of that. At the request of the Bangladesh Bank, the Federal Reserve Bank of New York blocked the remaining transactions, amounting to $850 million but we came away with a respectable amount.

Minutes before the heist, I had infected the Bangladesh Bank system with malware, which disabled the SWIFT printer. Bank staff initially assumed it was simply a printer problem, as this was a common occurrence. Because the international

SWIFT transactions were not printed, the fraudulent withdrawals from the bank's Nostro account went unnoticed until it was too late.

"I'll work from my hotel room," I told Uncle Zheng. "I'll go through the data you gave me and see if I can do something for you. Perhaps you could ask one of your sons to drop me off at my hotel."

The old man disappeared into his study. Returning, he apologized. "I'm sorry, all my sons are out at the moment, but I've called you a taxi."

I called Uncle Zheng at 11 pn that same day. "It's done," I told him. "I have access to the system."

16

The Arsonist

This was my second visit to the Mercedes dealership in downtown Shanghai. On my first visit I found out everything I could about one model's security system, now I needed to know about the car's air-conditioning unit. I even popped the hood and took photos. I was looking forward to this job. I'm a pragmatic person and will consider any job but I prefer to work under the radar of the authorities. This job ticked all the boxes and was out of China.

When I'd finished at the dealership, I visited the camping section of a department store and found a gas canister for a portable stove that would suit my needs. I didn't buy it but I took a few photos of it. After that I went up a few floors to the food court for lunch. I studied the photos as I ate my soup, then deleted them. I texted Bao Shen: "I'm ready."

Uncle Zheng

Jennifer gave me a demonstration of how she'd managed to retrieve the information from the gweilo's PC in Bangkok. She'd needed to travel to Thailand to complete the final step, she explained, emphasizing that she refused to do any work with amateurs. I said I would accompany her to Bangkok to oversee the operation, and this was the reassurance she wanted. We landed at Suvarnabhumi airport three days later. Unbeknown to us at the time, Bao Shen's arsonist was on the same plane.

Tony

To an outsider it might have appeared like a typical business meeting. Bao Shen sat timidly and kept quiet as Uncle Zheng took charge of the discussions. I liked the old man; he had style and spoke with a British accent. He stood up and leaned on his walking stick as he introduced his companion, a Chinese woman named Jennifer. She looked classy and charming, but I soon learned she had an arrogant attitude.

"What have you guys been smoking?" she asked. "What good is all this intel if you can't interpret it?" Her tablet was connected to a smart TV and she opened the files stolen from Hubert. I'd already scrutinized these files several times over the past few weeks. "This is an email Hubert wrote three weeks ago," she said. "You found it on Donald's smartphone. The message is of no importance, but look at it. It contains a date and time-stamp so we know exactly when Hubert wrote it." She opened another folder. "Now look at the files from Hubert's smartphone. The voice recording spyware was activated the same evening this email was written. We know from the spyware settings that the recording started at 7:13 pm that evening. Now we can run a timer until the moment that Hubert began writing the email sent to Donald."

She tapped a button on the tablet screen and I could hear the sound of someone typing on a keyboard. Every keystroke was highlighted on the TV screen over the text of the email. We sat in silence and watched as each keystroke we heard moved a coloured cursor across the text. None of us understood what she was getting at until she removed all the characters from the text except for the "A" key.

"Listen how the 'A' key sounds," she said. "We've finally got it – each key has its own sound like on a piano." She opened another audio file of Hubert typing away at his keyboard. "We don't have any corresponding text for this, but have a look at this!" She opened a programme that was able to reconstruct the text solely from the unique sounds that each keystroke produced. "Using this technique I've already found Hubert's account number and password for his Hong Kong bank account. We can get the one-time SMS password from the installed spyware in his smartphone, and then we can easily empty his bank account. That's the good news. The bad news is that Hubert has transferred most of his funds to a crypto exchange and bought bitcoin, which he always sends to a crypto wallet on his computer. I know this because he visits a blockchain explorer page on his smartphone to check his bitcoin transactions. I found the wallet address in his logs, and it currently holds a little over sixty million dollars in bitcoin." We all gasped. "Hubert probably didn't steal sixty million dollars," Jennifer continued. "The price of bitcoin went up twentyfold in the last few months."

"How can we be certain that these bitcoins are stored in only one wallet on his computer?" asked Bao Shen. "I have some stored in different online wallets."

"I doubt whether a criminal would store bitcoin in an online wallet with an exchange that the FBI or another government agency could get a court order for," Jennifer replied. "Besides, each time he buys bitcoin on an exchange I can hear him typing the same password, probably to check the updated balance of his wallet."

"All right," Bao Shen conceded. "We have the password to unlock his computer and bitcoin wallet, so we just need to break into his apartment and access his computer."

"How can we do that?" I asked. "The building's security is very tight. Visitors need to report to the front desk and are only allowed access after confirmation through a call with the resident who invited them. Even if I clear the visit, the front desk will register the visit to my name. Plus there are cameras in the lifts and landings on every floor. I doubt that even a professional burglar could gain access unnoticed."

"You could climb from your balcony to his," suggested Bao Shen.

"There are hundreds of condo units facing my side of the building," I said. "Even if I was stupid enough to try that, someone would call the police within a few minutes."

Jennifer cleared her throat and focused on the old man. "I delivered the access codes for the guy's bank account and bitcoin wallet. It seems to me that you lot need to work out how you're going to use that information."

Uncle Zheng

I didn't understand this business with the arsonist. There's nothing simpler than a bullet. It's clean and quick.

"Why would you hire an arsonist, Bao Shen?"

"It was his idea," Bao Shen replied, nodding in Tony's direction.

I listened intently as Tony explained the plan; applying torture and suffering is something that I could agree to, and Tony persuaded me that a bullet would just give Hubert an easy passage to the next life. I understood this American's desire for his enemy to suffer, since it wasn't strange to Chinese culture. I was aware of Tony's previous career, which made sense.

"Our interests don't conflict with yours," I told the American. "We just want to take out the competition and consider any money out of this deal as a bonus, so I don't see why we can't let these actions run simultaneously. But timing will be essential. I didn't bring Jennifer to Bangkok for sightseeing – she'll help both of us recover our funds without the need for an amateur break-in. Here's what I need you to do." I explained in detail the plan that would unfold over the following days.

Jennifer

I know I look good. My long silky black hair reaches down to my butt, and I know how to dress up. When I arrived by limousine to Tony's condo, the doorman took my luggage to reception.

"I'm moving in with my husband," I said. "Take my luggage upstairs."

"You are expected," the front-desk officer replied. "I have your keycard ready and you just need to complete this form while I take a copy of your passport."

I passed him the American passport Uncle Zheng had given me. The passport photo wasn't mine, but the resemblance was close enough, and the passport surname was the same as Tony, my fictitious husband.

Tony returned later that day. I'd set up what looks to the untrained eye an analogue TV antenna in the living room, and a portable parabolic antenna on the balcony. Both were connected to my laptop.

"All right," I said. "I'll show you how we're going to steal his private keys. The private key is like a secret number that allows bitcoins to be spent. Every bitcoin wallet contains one or more private keys that are saved in the wallet file. His computer and WiFi network seem unhackable, but thanks to our kinky friend Bao Shen, we have full-access control over his smartphone."

I opened a file to show Tony the list of Bluetooth connections in Hubert's smartphone settings. "His smartphone is linked to his computer, so I can send bridgeware from the smartphone to the computer. It will register his private key. His computer is about a metre above your ceiling. We'll receive his private key via the computer's magnetic radiation broadcast, either through the ceiling or the antenna on the balcony. Now we just need to wait for Hubert to log in to his bitcoin wallet."

17

Tony

Since moving to the new building, I usually ate at a food stall on the street just a few hundred meters away. The place served several different fried-rice dishes, which I enjoyed with a local beer. After Jennifer's arrival, however, I'd been accompanying her for dinner at upmarket restaurants. The food was good, but I didn't feel comfortable sitting between the high-society types and the wannabe "hi-sos". I missed my local street food, and brought the subject up a few nights later with Jennifer.

"I fancy getting some normal food," I said.

Jennifer raised an eyebrow in response. "You aren't inviting me?"

She smiled when I explained where I usually went for dinner.

"You seem to forget that I'm Asian," she said. "I'll come with you."

I guess you could say we both had dominant, albeit

opposing, personalities, but her remark managed to break some of the ice between us.

The following evening we went to the food stall. Jennifer appeared quite at home sitting on a plastic stool on the pavement, spooning her noodle soup while sipping a bottle of Chang beer, no less elegantly than she'd done with her glass of red wine the previous evening. It was the first time we had a meaningful conversation, and I outlined my plan in full to her.

The Arsonist

I'd checked into a decent hotel in Bangkok with a rooftop swimming pool and three renowned eateries. The hotel bar was always crowded with an international clientele. The room cost two hundred dollars per night – a bargain.

With the material specifications fresh in my mind, I located a hardware store where I bought a few tools, a small cooking-gas canister with a regulator, some flexible rubber hoses, duct tape, a three-way elbow connector and hose clamps. I then took a taxi to Chinatown for the electronics I needed. The Chinese shop owner nodded when I explained what I was looking for, and he disappeared into a small storage room in the back of the shop to collect the items. A little further down the street, I found a stall selling second-hand smartphones, and selected the oldest-looking one there. "I'll buy it if it comes with a new battery," I told the stallholder. After I had everything I needed, I took a taxi to one of the numerous short-time hotels in Chinatown, where rooms could be rented by the hour. "I'll get a girl later," I told the attendant as he handed me two towels, a condom and a bar of soap. The guy didn't seem to notice me and returned to playing a game on his phone. I climbed the stairs to my floor and unlocked the door; the room contained only a bed, a dirty bathroom, a fridge and a TV that was secured in a metal frame and bolted to the wall. I switched on the TV and was rewarded with very loud porn. I couldn't find a remote to turn the volume down, so set to work.

After removing the gas canister from my backpack, I opened the gas regulator and removed the valve, reducing the output pressure. I then replaced the valve with an electronic gas valve that had only two settings – fully open and fully closed. When activated, gas would stream out of the canister uncontrollably and empty the canister within a minute. I needed to operate the electronic valve remotely, so I modified the second-hand smartphone I'd just bought, soldering some wires to connect the phone to the electronic valve and a motorbike spark plug. On receiving a call, instead of ringing, the smartphone would activate the electronic gas valve, and then switch on the spark plug a few seconds later via a relay switch, using the phone battery to power both. To prevent it from being activated accidentally, I went into the smartphone settings and blocked all incoming calls except for a single number. I had to smile when I programmed the number into the smartphone settings, knowing that the police would check the origin of the call that activated the device; it would be a nasty surprise. I inserted a SIM card into the modified smartphone. It was from a country where proof of identity was not required when buying a preloaded SIM card. I went online and used a caller-ID spoofing app to make a test call.

Caller-ID spoofing

Nowadays almost all public telephone networks provide caller ID information, which consists of the caller's number and often the caller's name. Some Voice over IP networks allow callers to forge caller-ID information and present false names and numbers. This is known as caller spoofing. These false IDs are then forwarded to public networks; using this method it is possible to make calls appear to originate from other countries

The Arsonist

It worked perfectly; the smartphone didn't ring, but instead activated the electronic gas valve and the spark plug a few seconds later, exactly as planned. Now that both SIM cards were registered on a Thai network, the numbers and IMEI number were now stored somewhere in the records of a local telecom company. But I didn't worry as there was no way it could be connected to me, and Chinatown was far from my hotel.

I connected the gas regulator to the canister. Then, after screwing the three-way elbow connector to the opening of the regulator, I attached the spark plug to one of the other available openings of the elbow connector. The third opening would later be connected to the Mercedes' air-conditioning system. Next, using the duct tape, I taped the whole thing together and placed it in my backpack. As I left the short-time hotel, the attendant was still focused intently on his game.

Back in my real hotel room, I locked the backpack away in a wardrobe. I took a shower and changed into swimming gear then went up to the rooftop swimming pool. I sipped a cold beer and thought, not bad for a day's work.

One thing I still needed to complete the mission was a vehicle. A motorbike would be perfect on Bangkok's congested roads, but rental bikes required some ID, and buying a bike would involve even more paperwork. The following morning

I returned to Chinatown using the MRT to Hua Lamphong station, then hailed a motorbike taxi to take me to the Khlong Thom market. Walking to the Worachak intersection in the market, where spare parts could be had for almost every make of car and motorbike imaginable, I turned into a small side alley lined with Chinese workshops where men were dismantling motorbikes. Components were scattered over the shop floors, waiting to be cleaned and later sold at the nearby market. I greeted a man who was lingering at the entrance of a workshop, speaking to him in Mandarin.

"Are you looking for something in particular?" the man responded in the same tongue.

"I need one of those," I said, pointing to a motorbike in the process of being taken apart. "But I need one that is still intact. I don't need the original paperwork, though. Just give me something I can get away with if I get stopped on the road."

The man made no response, and I lit a cigarette. When I exhaled, the mechanic sniffed and I offered him one from the packet. It was a brand sold only in mainland China. The mechanic appeared a little more open when he realized where I came from.

"When do you want it?" the mechanic asked.

"Today would be good," I said.

"It'll take some time; come back in the afternoon."

Returning later that afternoon, I found the motorbike waiting for me in the back of the workshop. I'd already bought two motorbike helmets in different colours, and placed one under the seat along with some spare shirts, so I could change my appearance a few times to avoid being noticed by the target. I paid the Chinese mechanic and rode off to an apartment building near my hotel. Pretending to be a resident, I parked the bike next to a few others in the car park of the building and then walked back to my hotel.

The next morning as I was eating noodle soup at a food stall near Hubert's condominium block, I saw the Mercedes leave the garage. I didn't hurry my breakfast since I knew the car would be stuck in traffic within a hundred metres.

I got on my bike a couple of minutes later and set off in the direction of the car, spotting several traffic cameras along the route. As expected, the Mercedes had got stuck in traffic at a junction. A small police booth stood at the centre of the intersection, and I grinned when I noticed a set of traffic cameras on the roof. The cameras were positioned at different angles to catch incoming traffic from all directions. I knew this location could work, but I still needed to know if crossing this junction was part of Hubert's daily routine so I spent the next couple of days following Hubert's movements at the intersection.

I also needed to find out where I could work on the Mercedes and soon realized I'd have to work on it in the basement garage of Hubert's condominium block. This was the only place where the car was left unattended.

18

Ma Boxer

I had already visited Yayee in the hospital a few times. She was still in a coma and unaware of any visitors. I knew the nurse had shooed Tukataa away from Yayee's bed several times. Tukataa was in the same hospital but on a different ward, and as soon Tukataa was able to walk, she'd tried sneaking into Yayee's ward. The male nurse explained to me that Yayee probably had a blood clot on the brain.

"We'll have to wait and see if she comes out of it," he said. "The police have come a few times, but I had to tell them that an interrogation or transfer to the jail is out of the question."

"When will they come again?" I asked.

"They told me to call them if she wakes up or dies."

I looked at Yayee, lying comatose on the hospital bed with her face wrapped in bandages and I felt sorry for her. When I left the hospital I noticed a coffee shop in the lobby and ordered an iced coffee. The coffee shop overlooked the car park in front of the hospital. As I looked out the window, a pickup pulled up and an elderly couple got out. The old woman was crying; her husband attempting to comfort her. The couple left some time later. As they drove off, I noticed a coffin in the back of the truck. It looked like they'd come to collect the body of a loved one. As the pickup drove away, an idea started to formulate in my subconscious. I waited in the coffee shop until the same male nurse had finished his shift. When I spotted him crossing the car park, I approached him and made him an offer.

Tukataa

"Please wake up, Khun Yayee," I pleaded as I hugged Yayee's unresponsive, lifeless body. I know I had been annoying the hospital staff and had been caught wandering throughout the hospital on numerous occasions.

A ward nurse beckoned me with her index finger when she again caught me at Yayee's bedside.

"Come with me, *nong* [young lady]," she said. "We need to have a serious talk about your blood-test results."

Tony

It was Friday morning, and the moment had arrived. Jennifer had taken over the other bedroom after arriving in Bangkok.

She usually woke up late, but this morning she was already seated at the dining table when I got up. She didn't acknowledge me when I walked in and peered over her shoulder at the laptop screen. I saw that the bitcoin key receiver was active and I knew that the plan was nearing completion. I went into the kitchen to brew some coffee, thinking that Jennifer might need a cup or two as she was really more of a night owl. I returned holding two cups of coffee, but Jennifer was already disconnecting the wires from the antennas.

"It's done," she said. "Hubert just bought fifty thousand dollars of bitcoin, and I got his private key as soon as he logged in to his desktop bitcoin wallet."

It felt like an anti-climax as I stared at the jumble of letters and numbers on the laptop screen.

Later that day I entered the car rental office and approached the girl at the front desk. She tried persuading me to rent a Nissan March.

"Don't you have something bigger?" I asked.

After punching the keys on her keyboard for a few seconds, the girl said, "Yes, we have a Toyota Fortuner for you."

Half-an-hour later I arrived at the car park under my condo. The security guard opened the barrier and advised me to get a magnetic key card from the service desk. Once parked,

I went up to the lobby to complete a form requiring the car license plate number and some other details. I handed it to the girl, who in turn gave me a key card. Over the following few days, Jennifer and I moved the Fortuner in and out of the garage at random times, especially late at night, to ensure that the security guards got used to it coming and going.

Bao Shen called just before the weekend with the arsonist's instructions. The arsonist didn't want to be seen by a westerner, and so Bao Shen asked for Jennifer to pick him up in the Fortuner, insisting that she came alone.

Jennifer told me afterwards that when she arrived at his hotel the arsonist got into the Fortuner carrying a backpack containing the camping gas bottle he had rigged up with the regulator and the electronics he'd modified earlier. Jennifer also said she noticed the arsonist was wearing latex gloves. He would wear them until the job was finished.

Ma Boxer

As we expected, the male nurse reported the death of a female patient one afternoon shortly after I made him the offer, and it was evening by the time a doctor arrived to sign the death certificate. The young woman had been in the ward for almost two weeks and simply hadn't woken up after overdosing on yabaa. She hadn't had any visitors since arriving, which was not unusual for drug patients in Thailand. When the night shift started, the nurse brought a bag into the holding room for the deceased. He wrapped a towel around the recently deceased young woman's head, withdrew a piece of steel pipe from his bag, and then proceeded to hit the cocooned head repeatedly. He paused and unwrapped the towel to check the condition of the face. It was beyond recognition. He then re-wrapped the head in bandages and wheeled the body into the side ward where Yayee and a few other patients were sleeping. Earlier that evening he'd added some strong sleeping tablets to their regular medicines to ensure he could work undisturbed. He exchanged Yayee's identification tag with the deceased woman's, and then struggled as he transferred their bodies onto each other's beds. He then wheeled Yayee to the holding room where he carefully removed the bandages covering her face. She moaned despite being comatose. The nurse took no chances and injected her with a strong somnifacient to ensure she wouldn't react as he put her into a body bag. When he was done he phoned the morgue in the basement, "I have a new customer for you."

I was waiting in the hospital parking lot. I got a text from the nurse and drove to the morgue entrance. The nurse gave me some paperwork and told me to hand it to the man at the desk. The desk worker had a quick look at the forms and said, "Yeah, this one just came in." He didn't show much sympathy and just stamped my forms and scrutinized the receipt to ensure that I had paid all the hospital bills. "Everything looks OK," he said finally, "I'll help you collect your sister."

He wheeled Yayee out of the cold storage room and helped me lift her into a coffin in the back of my truck. I drove Yayee to a shophouse on a soi just off Pattaya Klang. On the ground floor there was a small family-run convenience store. I lifted Yayee onto my back and carried her to the rear of the shop and up three flights of stairs to the Lamsalee Sex-change Clinic. A little out of breath, I laid Yayee on a hospital bed as two nurses got to work on her. They began by removing her patient gown and they washed her, after which they covered her body with a sheet and left.

A doctor came over to me a few minutes later. "Are you sure? She might never wake up!" he warned.

"At least she'll die a man," I responded, "and if and when she does wake up, her wounds will be healed."

The Arsonist

After picking me up, Jennifer drove the Fortuner into Hubert's garage and held the key card over the barrier scanner. The dozing security guard woke up briefly before falling asleep again at the sight of the familiar SUV. I cursed under my breath as I noticed both parking spaces beside the Mercedes were occupied. I looked for the security cameras. Two cameras scanned the front row of parked cars, so I'd have to crawl in-between and under the cars to stay out of sight. I told Jennifer to park the Toyota as close as possible in the row behind the Mercedes. As Jennifer sought to find a space, I pulled out a disposable boiler suit from my backpack.

Before I could get out of the car, Jennifer turned to me and asked, "Why did you only want me to drive you into the garage?"

"I don't work with gweilos," I replied.

Jennifer stepped out of the car and I crawled between her legs and slipped under the Toyota. As instructed, Jennifer walked over to the lift in full view of the security cameras, and went up to the condo to wait there with Tony. I waited a few minutes after she'd left, and once confident I was alone, I performed a car-wireless fob-relay attack using the access codes Bao Shen had stolen from Hubert at The Gentlemen's Club. Opening the Mercedes, I crawled inside, stuck my head under the dash and got to work. I first used a small saw to cut the air-conditioning pipe that carried cold air into the cabin, and reconnected it using the three-way elbow connector, securing it with some hose clamps. I then pulled out another hose clamp from my backpack to attach the electronic gas regulator to the remaining opening. Next, I affixed the gas canister using duct tape, and was about to connect the electronic regulator to the gas canister when a car drove into the garage and parked not far from the Fortuner. I held my breath until the driver disappeared behind the closing lift doors. Once I felt safe again, I proceeded to connect the gas canister to the regulator using a piece of flexible pipe. I wasn't sure whether the smartphone battery would last long enough, so I connected a charger to the Mercedes electric circuit. I then hooked the smartphone to the electronic regulator and the spark plug. To create a good blast, it was important for the gas to mix with enough oxygen, so I inserted the spark plug inside the air blower. It was difficult to reach into the air vent from under the dashboard, and it took me nearly an hour before I managed to get it in position. The modified smartphone was left in airplane mode, otherwise it would be clear where and when it had been installed in the car. I'd installed an app called Tasker that would automatically bring the smartphone online again after three days, when Hubert's Mercedes would probably be in The Gentlemen's Club car park. I was confident that the police would assume the device had been installed there rather than at the condo. Although the fire would engulf the inside of the car, it wouldn't destroy the smartphone, meaning that forensics would be able to find it. To cover my tracks, I set up Android's lock and erase feature to remotely delete all the data once the job was complete. I inserted the phone into a gap within the wiring and secured it with some duct tape. After carefully checking that all the leftover materials and tools were back in my backpack, I carefully exited the car and locked it again, which reactivated the car's alarm system. I then crawled back to the Fortuner.

Once safely inside the Fortuner I sent a text to Jennifer, who came down and drove me back to my hotel. During the ride, I removed the disposable boiler suit and latex gloves. When Jennifer dropped me off it was almost light outside, but I didn't sleep, and a few hours later I was on a plane back to Shanghai.

Tukataa

I sneaked in to see Yayee again, but when I got there I saw hospital staff putting her body into a body bag. I couldn't move or breathe as they took her down to the morgue. I didn't cry though. I've witnessed death many times in my life already. I immediately left the hospital, desperate to escape, sad beyond words. My mind clouded over and I forgot to pick up the medicine I was supposed to collect from the hospital pharmacy.

19

Tony

Saladaeng intersection – one of the busiest in Bangkok – is connected to the BTS and the MRT lines. Jennifer and I arrived at a fast-food restaurant on the south-east corner of the junction shortly after rush hour. Jennifer went to order some drinks and I found a table by the window overlooking the junction. I wanted to see Hubert suffer.

Earlier that morning we'd used the remainder of Hubert's Hong Kong bank-account balance to buy bitcoin from his regular crypto exchange, and had sent it to his bitcoin wallet. The transaction didn't arouse any suspicions because it was identical to the many previous transactions between his bank account and the exchange, and then on to his bitcoin wallet. Jennifer had also created a new bitcoin wallet, and she was able to gain instant access to all his bitcoin by using Hubert's private keys. She immediately transferred all the bitcoin to the new wallet under her control. The whole process had taken less than ten minutes. I also asked Jennifer to record all the transactions made to the Hong Kong bank account since Hubert had opened it. I reckoned this information would help me trace the other victims of Hubert's investment scams.

We sat looking out of the window in anticipation.

The Arsonist

The smartphone hidden in Hubert's Mercedes had come out of airplane mode the previous day as planned while the car was in The Gentlemen's Club car park. The smartphone signal and IMEI number were registered for a second time with a Thai telecom company to suggest later that the device had been installed in the car at The Gentlemen's Club.

I loaded EarthCam.com on the laptop. I'd used it numerous times before on other jobs as it allowed me to see live feeds from cities around the world. I navigated to the Saladaeng intersection live feed to watch the images from the handful of roof cameras on the police booth. Since returning to Shanghai I'd used the website each morning to confirm the Mercedes was there at around the same time every morning. I also had TrapCall.com loaded on a second tab, from which anonymous calls could be made using any caller ID. I used the caller ID of a Saudi Arabian landline, the only whitelisted number

I'd programmed into the installed smartphone. I spotted the Mercedes pull up at the junction. I let the car continue until it was in front of Tony and Jennifer's restaurant before making the call. The Google account settings page associated with the installed smartphone was open on the third tab, from which I would use the lock and erase function to delete the smartphone data after activating the fire.

My work was done.

Tony

The Mercedes was so close I could see Hubert take my call through the car's hands-free system.

"It's time to answer for all the money you stole," I said. "You've destroyed a lot of lives." I could hear a sizzling sound in the car that would be the gas being released. "That sound you hear is gas. Soon you will be burning."

I saw Hubert's look of confusion turn to panic. I saw him try to unlock his door, but the arsonist had overridden the car's security system. I saw him desperately try to smash the windows using his bare hands, to no avail.

Suddenly a flash of fire filled the inside of the Mercedes, burning Hubert's hair in an instant, eyebrows and moustache gone just like that. The air-con continued blowing a mixture of burning gas and oxygen into the car. A second or two later, the air-con gas pipes and air vents melted, forcing the burning gas to be released under the hood and setting the engine on fire. The polyester in Hubert's shirt and pants melted to his skin. Then the fire stopped. The gas canister had emptied, but not before Hubert had second and third-degree burns all over his body. The skin on his legs and upper torso was black. I watched as he sat conscious and screaming in pain as the car filled with smoke.

The drivers of the cars lined up behind the Mercedes began honking their horns in frustration. I could see a policeman, who had been sitting in his police booth at the intersection, happily daydreaming, quickly grab his helmet. He left the booth and approached the Mercedes, now full of smoke. Then the cop ran back to his booth, picked up a fire extinguisher and smashed the Hubert's window. Smoke billowed out. Struggling to see through the smoke, the cop pulled Hubert out and laid him on the road. I could see from the restaurant that Hubert was beyond recognition. Most of his skin was charred and red, and his eyebrows and eyelashes had been burnt off.

20

Dividing the loot

Tony had been in touch with Maura in Kentucky, and she was a little surprised by his request. But once she realized that her clients and other victims would be reimbursed, she was quite happy to comply. Tony provided her with Hubert's Hong Kong bank account statements, dating back to when the account was opened.

Jennifer drove the Toyota to Suvarnabhumi Airport to pick up Uncle Zheng. The old man arrived on an early flight and so they reached the apartment before the worst of Bangkok's heavy morning traffic had appeared. He looked fresh and energetic despite the 5-hour flight, with nothing in his appearance to indicate that the old man had left Shanghai shortly after midnight. He asked Jennifer for coffee, and as they sat at the dining table he opened his luggage to remove a wrapped parcel. Uncle Zheng offered the package to Tony, "I brought something for you. I'm not good at finding suitable presents but Jennifer gave me some suggestions." Jennifer laughed in response. Tony tore open the parcel wrapping, finding it contained an old Blackberry smartphone with a physical keyboard below the screen. The smartphone had clearly been used as there were scratches all over the screen and back. A puzzled Tony looked at Jennifer. He knew that model went out of service years ago Jennifer laughed again. "Let me tell you a bit about this smartphone. I'll give you ten million dollars for it if you don't want it. It was bought second-hand a decade ago by a Chinese high-school student called Yang. He paid about two hundred dollars for it. It was his pride and joy, and the only valuable item he owned. He would hang out in internet cafés since he couldn't afford a computer at home. He eventually managed to save enough to buy a second-hand PC, but decided against it after reading an article about a new currency called bitcoin. He used his savings to buy two hundred dollars' worth of bitcoin instead.

"Back then, people stored bitcoin in wallets on electronic devices. Since Yang had only his second-hand Blackberry, he stored all his bitcoin in a wallet on it. That's the smartphone you're holding now. It can no longer make calls, but it has a WiFi connection and I can transfer the bitcoin stored on it to any bitcoin address you want. And it cannot connect you to the events that took place over the last few days – unlike Hubert's bitcoin, which are very visible on the blockchain, and require some extensive laundering through underground exchanges in China. That'll be expensive and time consuming for us, but if you accept this gift, we'll worry about that."

"Two hundred dollars in bitcoin?" queried Tony. Uncle Zheng smiled.

"The current value is close to thirty-five million dollars," answered Jennifer.

Fishing his smartphone out of his pocket, Tony scrolled until he found Maura's email. "Please send it to this address."

Jennifer left to work in another room and Tony turned to speak to Uncle Zheng alone. "You could have ripped me off. You could have kept the thirty-five million."

The old man smiled. "You are overlooking something important. Our business is a sensitive one. So long as we conduct our gambling operations outside China, my government will leave us alone. But stealing retirement funds from US citizens would only open a can of worms and jeopardize relations with the United States, and the authorities would close us down very soon."

A new life

Nid entered her apartment and left her grocery bags in the

kitchen. She was excited since John had proposed marriage and had given her a two-baht gold ring (about thirty grams). He explained they'd need to apply for a fiancée visa for Nid at the British Embassy, and asked to move in with her for the remainder of his holiday in Thailand. She undressed in front of the TV and walked over to the bathroom, throwing her clothes on the floor along the way. As she got in the shower, the late-night news showed the newly sworn-in Japanese Minister of Foreign Affairs being questioned by the Japanese and international press. The minister looked directly into the camera, his face resembling that of a toad. Nid had no idea that her first customer was being interviewed on international television. She applied some more shampoo and enjoyed the scent that filled the shower cubicle.

Tony

Carrying a bunch of flowers, Tony entered the private hospital and approached the front desk to ask where he could find his friend. Hubert had been placed in a private room. The burns on his torso, face and legs were covered in hydro gel, while his lungs had been severely damaged from inhaling the mixture of burning gas and oxygen. Tony walked to Hubert's bedside and crouched down to whisper into his ear, "I told you that you'd burn. Now I'm here to thank you on behalf of your investors. They appear quite happy with the return on their investments. Oh, and by the way, you'd better check your bitcoin balance and your Hong Kong bank account. I'm not sure there'll be enough funds left to pay for your hospital expenses."

Yuth

It was a typically beautiful Phuket morning. Tourists sunbathed and strolled along Patong beach, the same as on any other morning. Two young farang men both covered in tattoos, with their hair in tight knots and their faces covered by hipster beards, were arguing with a Thai man. These farangs were the type that hang around Thailand's tourist ghettos, acting as if they're worldly experienced travellers in an attempt to impress backpackers and other tourists. But here they stood arguing with a man who had rented them two jet skis. The Thai man had clear green eyes and a nose that had obviously been broken at some point.

"We didn't do this!" shouted the farangs as they pointed to the deep gouges on the bottom of a damaged jet ski. They'd believed they could talk their way out of it, but now a group of Thai men suddenly appeared and surrounded them. The farangs quickly realized they were in deep shit. This had become a daily routine to Yuth. Despite warnings plastered all over the internet, most farangs were just stupid and the jet-ski scam was a real money-maker. There was no doubt that the farangs would soon pay up. Yuth had settled into his new life remarkably quickly.

Yayee: Yuth

On waking up in the sex-change clinic, Yayee was upset to discover that her breast implants had been removed and her long hair cut short.

"You cannot be a beautiful girl anymore," Ma Boxer told her soon after she woke. "Look at your nose – it's even flatter than mine! And your face looks like you had a long Muay Thai career; longer than mine!" Ma explained how he'd lost nearly ten fights in a row, more or less ending his boxing career. A fan of his had offered him the opportunity of running a jet-ski rental business on Patong Beach. The price was too good for him to ignore, so he'd spent most of his savings on buying the business. "I spent a lot of money to get you out of this shit. Now you can work with me to pay it off," said Ma.

The investigation

Police Sergeant Wallop had recently been promoted from the

Royal Thai Police to the Department of Special Investigations (DSI). He was working on his first case in this new role, and was committed to doing his utmost to bring the assignment to a successful conclusion. He scoured the report laid out on his desk. At first sight, the fire appeared to be caused by a short circuit in the air-con system, but the police called the DSI after finding the remains of a smartphone, together with a gas canister and a spark plug hidden under the dashboard. The DSI detectives had managed to find out where the smartphone had been registered to the telecom's network, but the Gentlemen's Club parking lot had no security cameras as its clientele appreciated privacy and discretion. The spark plug was the type used in motorbikes, but that wasn't much help either because thousands of these were regularly sold in Bangkok. Attempts had been made to trace the owner of the smartphone they'd found melted under the dashboard, but the registered owner had sold it long ago. Confounding Wallop's investigation even further was the fact that the fire had damaged the memory chip to the point that it no longer contained any data. Nonetheless, the detectives had been able to scrutinize the call logs from several telecom companies, through which they were able to identify a landline number in Jeddah, Saudi Arabia. A few weeks had already passed since Wallop had submitted a request to foreign police agencies through the Thai Ministry of Foreign Affairs, as all such requests must go through that office. He'd emailed the ministry daily in the hope of expediting the case, but after not receiving any response, he picked up the phone and called the Foreign Ministry. He was first put on hold and then forwarded to several different departments. None of the people he spoke to were particularly cooperative. Finally, he was put through to someone who identified himself as the Director of Foreign Relations. "You can't keep asking these questions," the Director told him. "It's embarrassing and will get you nowhere."

"Why's that?" asked Wallop. "A crime has been committed and a man is fighting for his life in hospital. Why would the Saudis refuse to help?"

"Google is your best friend," retorted the Director before abruptly putting down the phone.

The Blue Diamond Affair: The Jewel Heist That Became a Diplomatic Nightmare

The Blue Diamond Affair, a series of events that poisoned diplomatic relations between Thailand and Saudi Arabia, was caused by a 1989 theft of gems belonging to the House of Saud by a Thai employee. The affair has soured relations between

Saudi Arabia and Thailand ever since.

In 1989 Kriangkrai Techamong was employed in Saudi Arabia as a servant in the palace of Prince Faisal bin Fahd. Kriangkrai stole US$20 million in gems and jewellery, including a valuable blue diamond, from the prince's bedroom and hid the stolen jewellery in a vacuum cleaner bag at the palace. He then shipped them to his home in Lampang Province, Thailand.

A Royal Thai Police investigation led by Lieutenant-General Chalor Kerdthes resulted in the arrest of Kriangkrai and the recovery of most of the stolen jewellery. Kriangkrai was sentenced to seven years in prison. However, thanks to his cooperation and confession, he was released after serving only three years.

Thai officials flew to Saudi Arabia to return the stolen items. But soon the Saudi Arabian authorities discovered that the blue diamond was not included in the returned loot and they discovered also that about half of the returned gems were not the stolen ones but fake replacements. Not much later the Thai media published charity gala photos where numerous wives of government officials were seen wearing diamond necklaces resembling those stolen from the palace. Of course this triggered Saudi suspicions that the Thai police and other Thai officials had taken the jewels for themselves.

Mohammad al-Ruwaili, a Saudi Arabian businessman close to the Saudi royal family, travelled to Bangkok to investigate. He disappeared on 12 February 1990, never to be seen or heard of again and is presumed to have been murdered. In addition, a few days before his disappearance, three Saudi Embassy officials were shot dead in Bangkok.

The murders remain unsolved, and no connection to the jewellery heist has been proven, but the Saudi government proclaimed that the Thai government had not done enough to resolve the mystery surrounding Al-Ruwaili's murder and that of three other Saudi diplomats.

Lieutenant-General Chalor was convicted and sentenced to death for ordering the 1995 murder of the wife and son of a gem dealer presumably involved in the affair.

The judgement was upheld by the Thai Supreme Court and Chalor was sentenced to death on 16 October 2009. Six other policemen were also convicted of involvement in the murders.

In 2002 Police Lieutenant-Colonel Pansak Mongkolsilp, who also was involved in the affair, was sentenced to life in prison. The term was upheld on appeal in 2005, but he was released in 2012.

Relations between the two countries deteriorated following these events. Saudi Arabia halted issuing work visas for Thais and discouraged its citizens from visiting Thailand. Diplomatic missions were downgraded to the chargé d'affaires level, and the number of Thais working in Saudi Arabia fell from 150,000-200,000 in 1989 to just 10,000 in 2008. This resulted in Thailand losing about 200 billion baht in annual remittances.

21

New York City: The Bronx

Lisa came home from the hospital at around 10 pm, still in her nursing uniform. Securing this job was an accomplishment for a black girl from the Bronx, but she still had to work extra shifts and do another job, looking after a retired couple, in order to support her elderly father. Unusually, her father was sitting in his armchair, waiting for her to come home. That morning, the old man had walked down a flight of stairs to collect the mail, taking twenty minutes to slowly climb back up the stairs with the stack of mail in hand. He put the letters down on the kitchen table and then began going through them. A few letters in, he came to an envelope carrying the logo of a law firm in Kentucky. He almost discarded it as junk mail, but his curiosity got the better of him and he opened the envelope.

"We are the executors of a now defunct investment fund in Hong Kong" the letter began. The old man recognized the name of the fund. A few years previously a smooth-talking salesman had persuaded him to make an investment over the phone. The salesman had convinced him that his investment would quickly go through the roof. When the firm became incommunicado, he went to the Bronx neighbourhood office of the Legal Aid Society, which confirmed what he had been afraid of. He'd been cheated, left to live off a small state pension while his daughter was forced to take on extra shifts and other jobs to help pay for his prescriptions.

"I'm pleased to inform you that your investment has dramatically increased in value" the letter continued. Attached was a cheque for $170,000. When Lisa approached her father, who'd been waiting for her patiently, the old man handed her the letter and cheque. She read the letter and the two sat in silence – they'd finally been given a break. Similar letters from the Kentucky law firm were received by others throughout the United States, Canada and the United Kingdom, leaving the recipients astonished and happy.

Maura

Over the past few weeks her life had changed dramatically. Her work had changed too. The usual legal work of divorces, insurance disputes and managing the miners' estates had certainly taken a back seat. She'd never been involved with the sale of cryptocurrency before, but it turned out to be a pretty straightforward process. She sold the bitcoin on a major exchange, and shortly after there was close to 35 million dollars sitting in her company account. Tracing down the investors was more challenging, however. Hubert's Hong Kong bank account showed their names and account numbers, but no addresses were available. Nonetheless, she'd eventually managed to track down all the investors. Tony wrote, instructing her to assess a four percent handling charge to the investors, reassuring her that all the investors would still be walking away with a tremendous return on their investments. When everything was settled, he had one more instruction, "Close up shop and come to me. I'm waiting for you."

Epilogue

The building stood tall on the banks of the Chao Phraya River, its construction had halted decades earlier due to the Asian financial crisis. The forty-nine floors were meant to be filled with condominium units as well as a shopping mall and a number of swimming pools, restaurants and wine bars. Tukataa sneaked into the deserted building through a gap in the metal fence and began climbing the concrete stairs. The HIV virus had already caused her to develop AIDS. Each day she suffered from fevers and headaches, and had rashes all over her body – her immune system had already given up.

It took Tukataa a long time to reach the upper floors. She had to pause to catch her breath several times on the way up, and by the time she'd neared the top, the sun was already setting. She found a space in what would have been the penthouse to plan her final escape. She carried with her a small bottle of Sangsom rum and enough yabaa tablets to bring down a water buffalo. She also brought a plastic cup she'd found in a litter bin in front of a McDonald's. After sitting in silence for a while, Tukataa picked up a discarded brick and crushed the tablets into a powder, which she added to the cup. Then she filled the cup with Sangsom.

As she sipped the mixture, Tukataa reflected on her life. She recalled her childhood, spent selling roses to tourists and washing car windscreens at traffic lights. Her mind then wandered towards the beatings in the orphanage and her subsequent life as a street prostitute. This life had not given her much. She was looking forward to the next one. When she felt on the verge of passing out, Tukataa swallowed the remaining mixture of rum, methamphetamine and caffeine. A cruise-boat passed by on the river far below. A live band was performing on the upper deck, while guests enjoyed the elegant buffet being served. Moments after her soul left her body, it floated over the cruise boat. Tukataa looked down and smiled, overwhelmed with happiness.

Dear Reader

Thank you for taking the time to read my first novel, *The Second Poison.* I hope reading it has given you as much pleasure as I got in writing it. If you liked this story, I would be very grateful if you took a moment to post a review on Amazon, Goodreads, or on one of my social media profiles that you can find through my website **pieterwilhelm.com.**

Pieter Wilhelm
Bangkok